THE
# HAUNTED
# BOOKSTORE
Gateway to a
Parallel Universe

Wagaya wa Kakuriyo no kashihonya san Novel 2
©Shinobumaru (Story)
This edition originally published in Japan in 2020 by
MICRO MAGAZINE, INC., Tokyo.
English translation rights arranged with
MICRO MAGAZINE, INC., Tokyo.

Seven Seas press and purchase enquiries can be sent to
Marketing Manager Lianne Sentar at press@gomanga.com.
Information regarding the distribution and purchase of
digital editions is available from Digital Manager CK Russell
at digital@gomanga.com.

Follow Seven Seas Entertainment online at
sevenseasentertainment.com.

TRANSLATION: Kevin Ishizaka
COVER DESIGN: Nicky Lim
LOGO DESIGN: George Panella
INTERIOR LAYOUT & DESIGN: Clay Gardner
COPY EDITOR: Jade Gardner
PROOFREADER: Meg van Huygen
LIGHT NOVEL EDITOR: E.M. Candon
PREPRESS TECHNICIAN: Melanie Ujimori
PRINT MANAGER: Rhiannon Rasmussen-Silverstein
PRODUCTION MANAGER: Lissa Pattillo
EDITOR-IN-CHIEF: Julie Davis
ASSOCIATE PUBLISHER: Adam Arnold
PUBLISHER: Jason DeAngelis

ISBN: 978-1-64827-661-3
Printed in Canada
First Printing: March 2022
10 9 8 7 6 5 4 3 2 1

# THE HAUNTED BOOKSTORE

### Gateway to a Parallel Universe

VOLUME 2

The Fake Family and a
Promise Made Under the Stars

WRITTEN BY

## Shinobumaru

TRANSLATED BY

## Kevin Ishizaka

Airship

*Seven Seas Entertainment*

# TABLE OF
# Contents

# A Promise Between Fake Family

WHEN I WAS LITTLE, whenever I had a sleepless night, Shinonome-san would take me to see the stars. We would go to a small hill a short distance away from town, perfect for its absence of both nearby dwellings and light, and burn some incense to clear away the glimmerflies, these pesky luminous butterflies that followed me around. Then we would stargaze to our hearts' content. Just the two of us, some lamplight, and the stars.

As we gazed at the stars, we would talk about books—as the proprietor of a bookstore and his daughter were apt to. Sometimes, we would even bring books that had stars as motifs, or illustrated encyclopedias of space, and we would discuss their contents in depth. My favorite book to talk about was one about a pilot who, in the middle of a desert, meets a prince from a faraway planet.

The planet the prince lived on, the other planets he visited, his unique perspective on Earth, and the beauty of his flower, one that I could just so vividly envision—it all left me spellbound.

The two of us would discuss the story at length with Shinonome-san giving his interpretations and me giving my own. At times, our interpretations differed, and we bashed heads, leading me to grow heated with frustration. But I always eventually cooled down, which allowed me to find our differing opinions intriguing in their own right.

Still, I was a child. No matter how intriguing our discussions were, when the time came, I was out like a light. Once I'd roused some, I would be greeted by the familiar feeling of swaying atop Shinonome-san's back as he walked home. I loved those moments.

I made a lot of memories atop that hill, but there was one that left an especially deep impression on me. I was five then, if I recall correctly. The end of summer was nearing.

"Summer is the color of fresh, crackling melon soda, and autumn is the color of sweet and sour grapes!"

"What's this about?" Shinonome-san gave me a mystified look.

From his lap, I looked up at him proudly and said, "The sky! Look, it's so pretty!" I pointed at the sky with my still immature hands and laughed. In the spirit realm, the color of the sky changed together with the seasons, something that awed me at the time.

The spirit realm was the world the spirits lived in. It was also a world of perpetual night. Even so, while nothing was quite like standing underneath a perfectly clear blue expanse, the sky of the spirit realm was beautiful in its own right, with its colors that shifted over time and the multitude of stars dotted across it.

We had brought a book about stars that day. I recall I was a bit worked up with excitement then, having just learned the magic behind the twinkling stars' colors, and said just that.

Shinonome-san's face scrunched up into a smile. "I see, I see. You come up with some amusing things, Kaori. Maybe you'll be a writer in the future?"

"Hmm... I dunno." I'd only been a reader up until that point, but the thought of making my own books sounded fun, so I grinned back and answered, "Maybe." I continued, saying, "What about you, Shinonome-san?"

"Me what?"

"Your future! What'll you be?"

The moment I said that, his face grew troubled, and he averted his eyes toward the stars. "Well...I'm already an adult."

I blinked a few times, genuinely confused. "Can you not become something once you're an adult?"

*Then maybe an adult wasn't something to be,* I thought to myself then. What would an adult who couldn't become something even do? Idle their days away doing nothing, forever and ever?

"That sounds boring..." Like a child does, I said what came to mind, unfiltered.

Shinonome looked surprised briefly, then smiled wryly. "It's not that it's too late to become something. It just takes courage to take that step forward once you're an adult."

"Being an adult sounds hard."

"I'd say it's more annoying than hard."

"Oh," I remarked as I looked up toward the sky again.

Today's cloudless sky was the color of melon soda. But I could see the color of grapes beginning to encroach in the far distance. That meant summer was ending, and autumn nearing. I was sad about the former, but I was also looking forward to autumn and the many yummy foods it would bring.

As I thought about it, I realized it felt like it had only just been the height of summer. At this rate, the seasons would pass me by in a flash, and I would be an adult before I knew it.

Would I manage to become *something* before then?

I felt a sudden pang of worry and clung to Shinonome-san.

"What's wrong?" he asked.

"Nothing." Touching him set me at ease, but I kept that a secret as I didn't want him to think I was still a little baby. That was when a flash of genius struck me. I said, "Okay, then, I'll help you if you ever find something you want to be."

"...Come again?" he asked.

"I don't know what you'll want to be, but I'll help you become it!" Having now voiced the thought, I became confident that it was a splendid idea. "I'm sure you'll need lots of help finding the things you need to become something. Important things, like... treasure! The fox in the book said it too, 'What is essential is invisible to the eye.' It might be hard...but two people are better than one. We can do it!"

A happy thought crossed my mind then. I had found it. I had found the *something* I wanted to become. I met his eyes and, with some excitement, said, "I'm going to become your real daughter one day! That way I can help you more!"

I was not a spirit but a human who had wandered into the spirit realm at the age of three. One summer day, I had found myself in this dark, dark world, hurt and afraid. It was a world abounding with spirits who loved nothing more than to snack on bawling little children like me, as many had apparently tried. If it weren't for Shinonome saving me, I'd likely have been somebody's meal long ago.

Shinonome was...peculiar for a spirit. Not only did he save me, he even chose to raise me after learning I had nowhere to go. But we were not blood related. I thought of him as a father, but I felt I would always lack something a real daughter would have.

But it was okay. I would become his real daughter. If I did, I'd surely be able to help him better—and if not that, at least I'd be allowed to stay by his side forever.

Without hesitation, Shinonome embraced me tightly. "Oh, Kaori, you silly, silly girl..."

"Eww, you're all pokey!" His unkempt stubble prickled my cheeks. I thumped against his chest in protest. "Let. Me. Go!"

"Oh, sorry." He released me, apologetic.

I puffed up my cheeks and glared at my inconsiderate adoptive father. "How many times have I told you that you need to shave your face?!" My cheek still stung from where his stubble had prickled me. I continued to complain until I noticed his eyes were moist. My anger then quickly faded, replaced with concern. "What's wrong?"

"You are my daughter," he said, a bit emotionally. "Even if we aren't blood related, you are without a doubt my daughter."

Saying that, he lifted me onto his shoulders. In an instant, I was high and the sky so close. I let out an exclamation of awe as I gazed up at the stars.

Quietly, he whispered, "I have no need to look for anything. I have what's important to me right here."

"Huh? Did you say something?"

"Nope, nothing!" He roared with laughter and then said, "All right, how about you lend me a hand if I ever find that something that I want to be?"

"Yeah! You can count on me!"

"Well, aren't you reliable!"

He suddenly began to run down the hill. Finding the thrill to be pure joy, I cried out for more. He gave just that, quickly increasing his speed. We soon left the range of the incense repellent, causing glimmerflies to appear and give chase. The speed at which he ran and the swarm of glimmerflies following behind made us look just like a shooting star.

"Aha ha ha ha! Faster, Shinonome-san, faster!"

"You got it!"

That moment at the end of summer, spent with my adoptive father on that starry hill, was a treasure I held dear to my heart. The wish I made then, that dream of mine—*I'm going to become your real daughter one day!* It persists to this day.

# CHAPTER 1

# In the Valley of Gangala

S UMMERS IN THE SPIRIT REALM were short. The moment that Obon—the festival of the dead—ended, the frigid air and chilly nights returned.

I wonder why we curse the summer heat so much yet feel a tinge of sadness once we realize it's gone. Perhaps it's because summer is special, resplendent and brilliant like the sun, and packed with memories as dazzling as the sea that glistens under beams of light.

This summer had been eventful to say the least: We'd found an injured former exorcist, Shirai Suimei, and taken him in. Then we went to Oboke Gorge in Tokushima to help Goblin's friend. After that, we convinced Suimei to lodge at our house while he looked for someone. While with us, he helped me deliver a book to Mount Fuji, tend to a pair of cicada spirits on their deathbed, and look for the owner of a bookmark. Finally, there had been an incident with a Jorogumo. It really had been an eventful summer.

Of course, the most impactful thing of all was meeting Suimei. The time we spent together had been full of meaning. The two of us—one raised in the spirit realm and the other in the human world—were different, but since our meeting, we had eaten, seen, and experienced many things together. He'd comforted me through my hardships, and I through his. He'd even saved me a few times.

Now, he worked at an apothecary located in the spirit realm and lived a fulfilling life together with his partner, Kuro, whom he had been searching for.

My eventful summer was nearing its end. What would autumn bring? The future was a mystery to all, and that made life worth living. But I knew one thing was for certain: Life in the spirit realm would be much livelier now, with Suimei thrown in the mix.

I let out a deep, longing sigh.

I was in the only bookstore in the entirety of the spirit realm, located on the outskirts of town. It was a two-story Japanese-style building far shabbier—ahem, far more *unique*—than the houses that surrounded it. It also doubled as my home.

"Suimei..." I sighed again. I was sprawled atop the low dining table located in the living room of our living space. The face of that white-haired boy, Suimei, was at the forefront of my mind. Thinking of him made my heart ache; speaking his name made my chest tight. I could deny the truth no longer—I needed him. Only with him by my side could I be at ease.

"Suimei...I need you..." I sighed again, feverish this time, and gazed into the distance. My eyes locked on to the kitchen cabinet, the sliding door of which was open just a smidge. From within, a slowly depleting rice bin could just be made out.

My heart leapt the moment I saw the rice. Unable to bear the aching any longer, I screamed forth the desires of my heart: "Suimei! I need your rent money!"

"Heh. You had me for a good moment there. You all right in the head, little miss?" I heard an aloof voice from behind me.

"Ah..." I turned around to see a quirkily dressed man standing behind me. He looked about Shinonome's age and wore round sunglasses, through the lens of which I could see his right eye was clouded. His peculiarly long, black hair was capped with a fedora, and he had facial hair that was well kept, unlike Shinonome-san's stubble. He wore a haori over an open-necked shirt and hid his right arm inside his clothes.

Every time I met this man, he had on a different haori, all equally quirky. Today, his haori was based on Edo-period *bijin-ga*—woodblock prints depicting beautiful women—and showed a woman covered in white face powder giving a flirtatious sidelong glance.

The man's name was Tamaki. He was an old friend of Shinonome-san's and someone I'd known since I was little.

I gave him a goofy smile and greeting. "Oh, hello."

"So... What was all that earlier?" he asked, furrowing his brows. I could hear strain from holding back laughter as well as genuine confusion in his voice.

Embarrassed, I answered, "No, see, if Suimei, um, if this guy who lodged here a while ago was still paying rent, we'd be able to fill our sorry excuse for a rice bin up with some A-grade rice, you see?"

Tamaki-san shook his head, then pushed up his glasses with a finger and said, "Phew, and here I thought you were suddenly gunning for a man out of the blue. I'm not a fan of such abrupt developments, not even in stories. You gotta stick to the formula, you hear?" He let out a deep, guttural laugh.

Likening things to stories was a habit of his. I apologized for saying misleading things and gave him, our guest, a cushion to sit on.

Our home was a bookstore, but not one profitable enough to make ends meet. That wasn't to say our bookstore wasn't popular; it very much was. But two factors kept our budget tight: Shinonome-san and the circumstances of the spirit realm.

Many spirits lived the old way of life, self-sufficient and without currency. Such was the spirit realm, a place where much of what was long lost from the human world still remained.

However, Shinonome-san, the bookstore's proprietor, still lent books to these penniless folk, and he collected interesting stories in place of money. There was a way to turn these stories into money...but it took time. Hence why we were always just scraping by.

I understood the feeling of not wanting to turn away spirits eager to read, I really, really did. But one had to know where to draw the line. If we couldn't eke out a living, then there would be no bookstore from which to lend books in the first place.

I took on a part-time job in the human world, but even then, finances were tight. That was why the rent Suimei paid while he stayed with us had been such a boon. Without him, our meals were back to the cheap stuff.

"I can bear not having the best meat, but rice is the core of my diet. I simply cannot go back to the budget rice blends after having tasted heaven. I'm thinking I might have to take up more shifts at my part-time job."

Tamaki-san flashed a somewhat warped smile. "Hmm... That idiot would be torn to hear this."

"Who? Shinonome-san?"

"Who else is there? I can imagine the face he'd make now. Yes, yes... How delightful. Go on, then, take up as many shifts as you can."

"That's...a bit mean to him, don't you think?"

"What's it matter? An overly doting father like him could do to learn some moderation. Besides, it'll likely lead to some interesting story developments." He stroked his well-kept chin hair and laughed gruffly. He then took a deliberate look around the room and asked, "So, where is he?"

"Hm? He should be back there... Huh?"

Shinonome-san's room was right next to the living room. Normally, he could be seen writing away with his back facing me, but at present, he was absent. I peered in further to see unfinished manuscripts scattered about, but still no sign of their author.

"Oh dear..."

"He turned tail, huh?" Tamaki-san clicked his tongue and then sat back down on the tatami. "I'll wait until he returns. Could I have some tea?"

"Oh, sure."

"He's a handful, that man; running away even though he knows he can never truly evade me. Just like how the villains in stories are always eventually caught."

Tamaki-san was a story-seller, an unconventional job that involved collecting stories and anecdotes involving spirits and later selling them. Such things were apparently in demand among folklore researchers in the human world. As I alluded to earlier, Tamaki-san was the buyer of the stories Shinonome-san collected in lieu of money. The payment we got from Tamaki-san was a vital source of income for the household...but Shinonome-san was a fatally slow writer, so things often ended up not working out.

Today, Tamaki-san had come to collect manuscripts, and Shinonome-san, having not finished, fled. All in all, nothing unusual for our family.

Feeling somewhat apologetic, I brought tea to Tamaki-san. "It's nothing much, but here."

"This house *actually* had some high-grade tea leaves? How unexpected. I feel as surprised as I would if I'd just incorrectly guessed the culprit of a mystery novel."

"Ugh. I see you're as blunt as ever."

"I pride myself for my honesty," he said, happily drinking the tea.

*I just don't get you...* I'd known Tamaki-san since I was old enough to be aware of my surroundings, but not once had I managed to get a read on his personality. Was he kind? Was he mean? Even now, I was left guessing. What's worse, his character shifted from time to time, leaving me at a loss as to how to act toward him. Today, he seemed a bit irate, but that much was completely understandable after Shinonome-san missed his deadline and bailed.

As I was thinking such things, Tamaki-san said, "Oh, that reminds me. There's been something I've been meaning to ask you."

He squinted at me with his clouded right eye. It was unusual for the well-learned story-seller to have something to ask me. I turned to face him, and he locked on to me with that foggy gaze.

"I heard the rumors. That Suimei person you mentioned...is a former exorcist, right?"

"Right. We let him stay here for a while after he wandered into the spirit realm all injured."

"I see..." he said, before dipping into thought for a short while. When he finally did speak again, he chose his words carefully. "I heard he was...bound to an Inugami?"

"Yup. The reason he came to the spirit realm in the first place was to look for his Inugami partner."

"Oh?" Tamaki-san leaned in, urging me to continue.

I was a bit bewildered by this new behavior Tamaki-san was exhibiting, but I continued regardless. I talked about all the twists and turns the pair had experienced leading up to the incident with Jorogumo, and how their bond had for a moment seemed irreparable, but that it was eventually restored, leading to their choice to live together.

"I see..." Tamaki-san wore a thin smile. He then asked me a most unexpected question. "I take it the exorcist has been freed of his ancient bindings?"

"Huh? Ancient what-now?"

"The foolish customs restricting that Suimei fellow; he's free of them, no?"

"O-oh. Yeah."

The ancient bindings Tamaki-san was referring to were the intentional suppression of emotions that those bound to Inugami had to endure. Inugami could bring a family great fortune, but not without a cost. If someone bound to an Inugami were to feel jealousy toward another, that person would be cursed with ruin, sickness, and pain. So, to continue enjoying the fortunes the Inugami brought, their users suppressed all their feelings, as any stray emotion might inadvertently lead to jealousy.

It was an abhorrent practice, one that had deprived Suimei of a very basic right. Thankfully, it was all in the past now.

"Hey, Tamaki-san. How do you know so much about those bound to Inugami and their practices?" I asked, curious. Such things weren't widely known, after all.

Due to the nature of their work, exorcists were often hated by spirits. Tamaki-san was a long-lived spirit, even if he took the form of a human now. He wasn't as simpleminded as Shinonome-san either, and his thoughts were complex and hard to read. If, by some chance, he had a grudge against exorcists, things might become problematic.

I felt a shiver run down my spine and cursed myself for thoughtlessly talking about Suimei. I swallowed, then timidly asked, "You're not thinking of doing anything strange to Suimei, are you?"

Tamaki-san brought his teacup to his lips and said, "I haven't the faintest idea what's made you so apprehensive. I am a story-seller. I collect stories and anecdotes about exorcists all the time. Naturally, that includes those of Inugami exorcists."

"Ohhh. Of course." A wave of relief washed over me, and I smiled. At the same time, I felt shame for doubting a close friend of Shinonome-san's.

"Oh, right, right." Tamaki-san seemed to remember something out of the blue and began rummaging through his bag. "I almost forgot. Rejoice, for I have brought your bookstore more work. No need to rejoice as much as a bookworm receiving their first book of the year."

He handed me a single manila envelope. I looked inside to find a list of spirits who wanted to borrow books, the names of the books they wanted to borrow, and a bunch of other information of dubious relevancy—all written in neat and compact lines.

"Uh... Am I supposed to just deliver these books to them?" I asked.

"Well, I don't know."

"Huh? But aren't you the one who brought this list to me?"

I could feel Tamaki-san peer at me through his sunglasses.

"The one who received these orders was me, but the one who decides how to fulfill them is you. All the information you need is there. Whether you spare no effort or give none at all is your choice. You can work according to the requests' rewards or even wait until you have spare time. It's all up to you."

He then took his teacup, tilted his head back, and drank it dry. "You're free to interpret *everything* as you like. That is all."

I gave the order forms in my hands a good, hard look and calmly thought over Tamaki-san's riddle-like words. I then decided I would undertake the work. "Got it. I'll give it a shot!"

"Very good. Oh, and one more thing..." He slowly stood and walked over to the closet in Shinonome-san's room. In one swift motion, he slid the closet door aside and said, "I'll be borrowing this man until he finishes his manuscript."

The closet opened with a smooth, gratifying sound to reveal Shinonome-san, crammed into a space far too small for his body. He looked even more ragged than usual, perhaps on account of the small space, and he smiled awkwardly as he raised a hand. "H-hey... So I'm actually against that whole Kaori taking on more shifts thing from earlier..."

Tamaki-san and I both let out a weary sigh, before moving to catch Shinonome-san as he tried to flee.

Several days later, one of the dates listed on the order form had arrived, so I went to a back-alley street in a corner of town. It was an unremarkable and gloomy street, with nothing but a dilapidated door at the end of it. There, I waited for my friends.

The day's job would have been a bit much for me alone, so I figured I might as well get the whole gang together.

I played with the fluttering glimmerflies and waited. Eventually, a lone black cat approached.

"I can't believe you. You'd seriously go that far just to lend books?"

It was Nyaa-san. She glared at me with her mismatched eyes, one sky-blue and one golden. Her three tails restlessly waved in the air, a sign that she was in a foul mood. She was a Kasha spirit and my dear childhood friend. We'd been together since youth, so it was no exaggeration to say she was family. She knew me better than I knew myself, corrected me when I erred, and always tagged along for adventures—even if she did complain all the while.

"Sorry, I guess?" I said.

She shook her head and sighed. "You'll go even if I try to stop you, so I might as well tag along."

"Nyaa-san!" Overjoyed, I hugged her. I spun her around in circles and shoved my face into her, then inhaled until my lungs were full of the smell of her sunbaked fur, causing her to thrash.

"You know I don't like to be touched without permission!"

"Right. Sorry. I got carried away." I put her nose to mine and smiled.

Her face grew conflicted, then she let out a deep sigh before licking my nose with her rough tongue. "Well, they'll probably have some tasty fish over there... All right, brush me once we get home, serve me some of that higher-end canned food, and no cutting my claws for the time being. Got it?"

"Got it. I'll bring out some of that extra special canned food I've been saving."

"Promise?"

"Promise."

The two of us giggled. That was when Kinme and Ginme arrived.

"That's Nyaa-san for you, always the clever one. I'm really looking forward to this trip. I've been wanting to go for a while now," Kinme said.

"Yeaaah! I can't wait!" Ginme said.

In contrast to Nyaa-san, who was making a sour face, the two twins looked as happy as could be. They were childhood friends of mine, like Nyaa-san. The easygoing one with sleepy golden eyes was Kinme, and the rambunctious one with cheery silver eyes was Ginme. They were raven Tengu spirits. Unlike most spirits though, they were younger than me, and so they regarded me like an older sister, and I regarded them like little brothers.

The pair loved anything fun and had gleefully offered their help when I told them where I was going. They had arrived wearing differently colored aloha shirts, as well as swimming trunks, float rings, and snorkeling goggles—in other words, they were fully decked out for a swim.

"I wonder what kind of food they've got over there. Let's make sure we eat lots and lots, Ginme."

"Oooh, I wanna go to the beach, and go diving, and go see the Blue Grotto, and go to the coral reefs, and everything!" Ginme then gave me a sidelong glance and blushed. "Hey, Kaori, you got some time after this job? I was thinking we could hang out together afterward for a bit. I-I hear there's this place that looks real nice in the evening. How about it? Just you and, um..."

"How about the three of us all go together?"

"K-Kinme, you idiot! It's supposed to be just Kaori and me!"

Kinme sadly slumped his shoulders, turning his back to Ginme and muttering, "Oh, I see. I'm being left out... Aww..."

"What?! No! That's not it!" Ginme protested through teary eyes. Kinme, on the other hand, was actually smiling where his brother couldn't see. He enjoyed messing with his easily teased twin.

"What close brothers," I said, watching with a smile. That was when I heard a sigh. I looked to see a white-haired boy standing there with a fed-up look on his face.

"Your bookstore's free to take business trips, but do you have to drag me along?"

"Suimei! You came!"

"Not because I wanted to."

This was the former exorcist I had discussed with Tamaki-san. He looked as though he had been conjured from the lightest of pigments, with his pure-white hair, light-brown eyes, and skin pale enough to glow. He definitely would have been a hot item with women if it weren't for his somewhat sour personality and awkward self-expression. Last I'd checked, he still had problems with emotions.

He grumbled something about Noname telling him to come, making me think there was a good chance that Noname—his employer at the apothecary—had half-forced him to come. She was pushy like that sometimes, something I knew well; she was the one who'd raised me in place of a mother. I could easily see her telling Suimei to go off and make some nice summer memories without leaving room for rebuttal.

"Did you get forced into this? Sorry," I apologized, genuinely feeling bad.

His frown was conflicted. "I wasn't exactly *forced*, but still... This is way too far a trip to make just to lend books."

Suimei was about to continue his complaint, but he was immediately cut short by another ecstatic voice.

"Yahoo! Yahoo! This'll be my first time traveling to the southern islands!"

"Kuro, settle down—"

"Have you ever been there, Suimei? You haven't?! This'll be a first for both of us then! Okinawaaaa!"

The owner of this ecstatic voice was Suimei's partner, Kuro the Inugami. Kuro looked like any other dog at first glance, but being an Inugami, he had some traits that made him distinct. His body, covered in black fur and red spots, was a bit too long for a dog. One could easily mistake him for a weasel if it weren't for his head being too large and his ears too pointed. Of course, above all else, the most distinct thing about him was that he could talk.

Kuro coiled around Suimei's leg, his crimson eyes sparkling with excitement while his pink tongue hung from his mouth. "Hey, hey, are you excited too?!"

Suimei looked down at Kuro—who was ecstatic to the point that he swung not just his tail but his hips as well—and froze. A bead of sweat rolled down his face. Eventually, he carefully picked up Kuro and said, "Yeah. Can't wait."

"I knew it!"

This was Shirai Suimei. At first glance, he appeared to be the calm and collected sort, but he was actually a complete softie for his dog.

"I get the feeling you're thinking something incredibly rude right now..." Suimei glared at me as though my thoughts had been laid bare.

"Not at all," I hurriedly denied as I walked away. I scooped Nyaa-san up into my arms and peeped back at Suimei to see him dutifully listening to Kuro ramble. A gentle smile graced the boy's face; not a shadow of the customs that once shackled him remained.

*Thank goodness...* I felt genuine relief from the bottom of my heart. Then Nyaa-san slipped out of my arms.

"Can we go already? Okinawa's pretty far." She walked up to the nearby dilapidated door and looked back at me with impassive eyes.

"Right. Let's get going."

Our destination was Okinawa. *The* Okinawa, famously ideal vacation spot. The spirit who'd made the order was unique to Okinawa as well, so there was a lot to look forward to.

Kuro, still in Suimei's arms, asked, "So, how are we getting to Okinawa? It's an island, so maybe by plane? Boat? Are we going to go to an airport or dock now?"

*Ah, déjà vu.* Nyaa-san and I exchanged glances and giggled.

Suimei looked lost for words as he looked down at his partner, so I said, "We're not using the human world's public transportation. Who knows when we'd get there if we did, and it's already too late anyway. Besides, where would we get the money?!"

At this, Kuro looked even more confused. "Then how are we going?"

"Isn't it obvious?" I thrust open the dilapidated door before us. Cold, white flakes instantly fluttered toward us from within as chilly air brushed my skin, giving me gooseflesh. I reflexively steeled my body.

Beyond the door lay hell, specifically the seventh of the Eight Cold Hells—the Hell of the Crimson Lotus. Its chill froze not only the bodies of the dead but their screams and souls as well. The skin of the damned souls trapped there was rent open by the cold, leading their blood to freeze into what resembled a crimson lotus flower, hence the name.

Kuro looked frightfully into the hell, then at me. "You're kidding."

"Nope," I replied. I firmly grasped Suimei's arm. "Oh, right. You were unconscious when you passed through here before."

I smiled and began to drag both of them into hell. "Well, better you learn now than never. The spirit realm and hell are connected. In hell, space-time can be a bit warped, and the laws of physics are sometimes reversed. That's why traveling to someplace far away, like Okinawa, can be done super quick by going through it."

"S-Suimei?! She's joking, right?!" Kuro looked to Suimei for help, but his master could only shake his head in defeat.

"That's just how things are in this world. You're going to have to get used to it."

"Wh-what's with that look of enlightenment?! Just what in the world have you gone through?! Nooo! I don't wanna go to hell! Nooooooooooooo!" Kuro's shrill scream echoed throughout our grim destination.

In an instant, piercing cold air enveloped our bodies.

We arrived in a dense subtropical forest. The twittering of birds I've never heard before reached my ears, and I was surrounded by unfamiliar fauna that strove toward the heavens to spread their leaves. Moisture clung to those leaves, making them appear a deeper, more vibrant green as they layered over and masked any path a would-be traveler might take.

This place, practically a jungle with all its teeming life, was known as the Valley of Gangala. It was located on the southern part of Okinawa's main island and had once been the site of limestone caverns, hundreds of thousands of years ago. Said limestone caverns had collapsed over the passage of time, leaving a lush, verdant valley in their wake, one that had at some point been inhabited by the Minatogawa hominids of the Paleolithic era.

The valley was roughly the area of Tokyo Dome and had been opened to the public in 1972, but due to a pollution-related incident, it had been sealed off only a few years later until the river environment could heal. Reopened in 2008, it remained open to this day, but only for guided tours—no regular entry. Perhaps because of those circumstances, many ancient spirits made it their home.

"I'm counting on you, Nyaa-san."

"Yes, yes."

Nyaa-san's body creaked as she quickly changed from a size able to fit in my arms to the size of a tiger. Flames coiled around her feet, and she stretched, showing off her supple body. I fastened the many bags I'd brought onto her, reminding myself to splurge on some extra-luxurious canned food to make it up to her later.

"Let's proceed quietly, everyone," I said.

We set off, staying off the intended path so we wouldn't be spotted by any tourists or tour guides. After proceeding in silence like that for some time, doing nothing but swatting aside the leaves taller than ourselves, we stepped onto a path bordered by two rugged, sheer cliffs. On one of the cliffs draped an enormous banyan tree that one couldn't help but look up at.

"Whoa... It's huge."

"Holy. It's ginormous!"

Kinme and Ginme expressed their awe at what was known as the "Sage of the Forest," a banyan tree said to have lived for over five hundred years that was affectionately considered the lord of the Valley of Gangala.

Suimei looked up at the tree towering over us from the cliff edge. "It's incredible. What are all those things on it? Vines?"

"Those are aerial roots," I answered. "Some trees are like that."

This banyan tree was enormous, but the majority of it was actually aerial root, not trunk. What trunk it had extended aerial roots down the cliff like a cascading waterfall. The aerial roots that reached the earth below became supports that helped the trunk prop up the tree's weight. All in all, its height was around twenty meters, the tallest known tree in all of Okinawa.

"Banyan trees are sometimes called the trees of happiness," I said to Suimei as the piece of trivia suddenly came to my mind. "Know why?"

"Hmm... Is it because they look like they're carrying down happiness?" he guessed. "This one looks more like a grumpy old man to me, though."

"Aha ha, I can kind of see that, with how the aerial roots hang down like hair. No, the reason has to do with the spirit that lives in banyan trees." As I spoke, I took something out from my bag: the order forms I had received from Tamaki-san. After confirming the contents of the one in question, I took a stick and drew a circle on the ground, then scattered another thing I had brought along.

"What's that white stuff?" Kinme asked.

"That's flour, right? But what for?" Ginme wondered.

I glanced up to see Suimei and Kuro also watching me curiously. Being the center of attention so suddenly left me embarrassed. "J-just a moment!"

I put some incense in the center of the circle and was done. "This is a traditional Okinawan ritual used to see the footprints of a certain spirit. You're normally supposed to do this in a dark place, but...I'm sure the lord of the valley will invite us in. The one I'm here to see is the spirit in the banyan tree, after all."

After telling everyone to move back a bit, I shouted at the circle. "Kijimuna, saatakamahi!" This was an Okinawan spell that translated to "Kijimuna, I've brought you sugar."

The effects were immediate. Bright onibi-like lights appeared from thin air, drifting aimlessly for a moment before moving inward, toward the circle's center. Then, lo and behold, on the white powder I'd scattered beforehand, a small footprint appeared, like that of a child.

The footprint was alone for a few moments, until suddenly more appeared, running off in a direction. I hopped onto Nyaa-san's back and shouted, "Follow those prints!"

"Try not to get left behind, mutt."

"Humph! Who are you calling a mutt, cat?!"

"Hey, wait up, Kaori!"

"Looks like we better start running, Suimei."

"Whoa! This is getting me pumped!"

We followed the white footprints as they caked the ground, moving deeper and deeper into the forest. Gradually, the density of the surrounding banyan trees rose, and we had to jump, dive, and slip through the meandering maze of aerial roots to proceed. It must have been some twenty-something minutes before we reached a small clearing.

We were in a forest of banyan trees. They were everywhere you looked, and they varied in size, but towering over them all was a single banyan in the center. Perhaps, once upon a time, it too had been small, but over the years its aerial roots had grown unfettered, forming complex knots and overlapping to become the titan it was today. Between its roots were numerous small hollows, making it look like a house plucked straight from a children's book. My heart was tickled by the fairy tale quality of the scene.

Kuro spotted something to the side and shouted, "Suimei, look, look! There's fish swimming!"

"Huh? What are you..." Suimei followed Kuro's gaze and let his jaw drop.

Here and there, pouring out of the shadows and hollows of trees, were vibrantly colored tropical fish. They swam through the air as though the forest itself were their aquarium. The rounded green leaves of the banyan trees fluttered in the wind like aquatic plants, and together with the richly shaded fish, they formed quite the picturesque tableau.

A school of fish, big and small, swam past me just close enough to reach out and touch. *If I were to visit the Palace of the Dragon King from Urashima Taro's fairy tale,* I thought, *it would surely look something like this.*

"Hello! I'm here from the bookstore!" I hopped off Nyaa-san's back and called out. Nobody replied, though I could feel eyes watching me from all over.

Just then, someone appeared from within the great banyan tree in the center. At first glance, they appeared to be a child. But their hair was a vivid red, and their skin was as copper-brown as

Ryukyu roof tiles. On their waist was a skirt made from grass, and their body was somewhat disproportionate with their arms, which were just slightly too long.

They were a Kijimuna spirit, the same kind of spirit I had traveled all the way to Okinawa for on a request.

"Mensore, and thank you for comin'." After a bow, the Kijimuna flashed a toothy smile.

As if that were the signal, a number of similar-looking people popped their heads out of the hollows of the great banyan tree.

"Mensore!" they cried in unison.

They then excitedly descended from the tree and crowded around us.

"Wh-whoa, whoa, whoa?! Um, h-hello?" I ventured.

"Nee-nee, we've been waitin' for ya!"

"Haisai!"

"Haitai!"

I became flustered, overwhelmed by the Kijimuna calling out to me with Okinawan words I didn't understand. I froze, unsure of what to do as they curiously pulled at our clothes and bags.

"Eek! Don't pull my tail!" Kuro was on the verge of tears after being mobbed by the Kijimuna.

Before I realized it, Kinme, Ginme, and Nyaa-san had escaped to the skies. Suimei was left on the ground, equally as helpless as I.

*Just what is going on?!*

While I was still at a loss, the first Kijimuna approached and said, "I'll be countin' on your help today!"

Half in tears, I pleaded, "Could you do something about these guys first?"

The Kijimuna were Okinawan spirits that were also known by many other names, including Kijimun and Bunagaya. They lived in old trees like banyan, sea fig, fukugi, and chinaberry, and they generally had child-like bodies, as well as red faces and hair. They were known for their love of pulling pranks; they might trick people into eating red clay disguised as red bean rice or get people stuck in tree hollows that were normally too small to enter. Quite the mischievous spirits.

At the same time, they were also known for bringing happiness to homes in which they took interest. As such, Okinawan fishermen practically always planted banyan trees at their homes for good luck—and because Kijimuna were known as spirits that helped with fishing.

Conversely, if someone angered a Kijimuna, they would be met with all kinds of misfortune. Some stories even ended in offenders losing their lives.

However, there was one thing that made them remarkably similar to humans: they formed families.

Once the sun set, stars twinkled across the sky, and the forest of banyan trees stood still in the dark, with nothing but the pupils of nocturnal beasts to light it. Even the air-swimming fish slept as the entirety of the forest waited with bated breath for the coming dawn.

Such was a typical night in the forest. But tonight was no typical night. Even long after the sun sank below the horizon, the forest was filled with light. Today was the birthday of Ami, a Kijimuna girl.

Decorations dotted the forest, and the onibi made by the Kijimuna had been placed everywhere for light. Tropical flowers littered the earth, and the plucking of a sanshin, a precursor to the shamisen, could be heard. Schools of fish danced to the rhythm, as did the Kijimuna themselves as they drank. Everyone smiled and sang and danced, celebrating Ami's special day with all their heart.

Before the great banyan tree was the main grounds of the celebration. There sat Ami, the star of the day. She wore a flower crown woven from hibiscus and a dress made from leaves, and she received everyone's congratulations with a smile. She did not speak, however, as she'd caught a cold some time ago and still had a sore throat.

A line of delicacies lay before her, the majority of which were made from fish from Okinawa's coastal waters. We were allowed to partake in the dishes as well and thoroughly delighted in the soft, rare fish meats.

There was deep-fried double-lined fusilier fish, steephead parrotfish in vinegared miso, some large saw-edged perch fish broiled with salt, fried fish cake, erabu black-banded sea krait soup, and more.

"Whoa!" Kuro exclaimed. "What's this erabu stuff?! I've never had anything like it! It's plump and chewy, but *utterly* flavorless!"

"Is...that a good thing?" Suimei mused.

"Oh, but it's delicious in soup. You should try it, Suimei!"

"I think I'm good." Suimei, knowing the soup's meat came from a sea snake, quickly declined Kuro's offer.

Seeing this, a Kijimuna approached. "Do you not like erabu? Then what about this?"

"Uwaaauugh!" Suimei recoiled on sight. The Kijimuna had brought over a heaping plate of fish eyes.

Kinme and Ginme swooped over, grinning.

"Oooh, lucky you, Suimei! Make sure you eat it all up!" Ginme said.

"Did you know Kijimuna really like eating the right eyeballs of fish? Anyway, here's a spoon," Kinme said.

"No, stop it! If it's so great, why don't you two eat it?!"

"No way," they chorused together.

Suimei treated the twins rather coldly; perhaps he was self-conscious about being so much shorter than them? Regardless, the twins continued to pester him like a friend, claiming that he was fun and that he acted as the straight man for their jokes.

"Looks like they're having fun." I watched the three squawk at each other as I took it easy, enjoying my food alone. Kuro ate his food in a trance while Nyaa-san snuck up behind him with a thrashing sea snake in her mouth. I could expect more hilarity to ensue soon.

Suddenly, the first Kijimuna from earlier approached. I knew him now as Ami's father, Kumu. He sat down next to me and looked over at Ami, still happily enjoying her birthday. "I'm counting on you for the next event," he said.

"Don't worry, I came prepared. I'll make this the best birthday ever."

He grew silent, his face on the verge of tears.

"What's wrong?" I asked.

"Nothing, I just...feel a little sad is all."

"Sad...?" I asked, confused as to why he would feel sad on such a happy occasion.

"That girl's an adult starting today."

"Really? How old is she?"

"Five."

"That's...young."

"Maybe to you humans, but not to us Kijimuna."

Kijimuna had male and female genders and formed families, both fairly uncommon things amongst spirits. Apparently, there were even tales of Kijimuna marrying humans. Anyway, it was tradition for Kijimuna women to begin preparations to marry after coming of age.

"Ami is the most beautiful girl in the forest. I'm sure she'll find someone to marry right away." Kumu sighed deeply before continuing. "She's loved books ever since she was a child, treasuring the few that washed up on our shores. For a long time, I've wanted to at least let her read as many books as she wanted, before she became of age and got married."

And so, Kumu had met Tamaki when the story-seller stopped by Okinawa. Once he learned of Kumu's circumstances, Tamaki said he'd introduce our bookstore to him, leading to the present situation.

"As a father, I wanted to do something for Ami; I wanted to give her a memory she would never forget even after she married. After all, what father doesn't want to give their daughter something special? I'm happy I can do just that now, but still... the sadness still lingers."

Kumu looked at his daughter, smiling and surrounded by people. "Will she be happy?" he wondered aloud. "Will she find someone nice to make a family with? I know there's no use in worrying at this point, but I just can't stop."

I could tell he truly treasured his daughter. An answering pang rose in my chest. "The worries of a father never pass, do they?" I said.

Kumu's face scrunched up into a smile. "No, no, I'm just a doting fool who felt he had to do more for his daughter to make up for a lack of a mother. Thank you for helping by bringing your books." He looked at me head-on. "You people are invaluable to us spirits. It's hard for us to come by books, you see."

He began talking, detailing how spirits like himself found the ever-changing humans they shared the world with fascinating and wanted to learn more about them. Of course, what better way was there to do that then through books? But for spirits who lived in the forest, mountains, and seas, maintaining a book through winds and rain proved a constant struggle.

"Truth is, we'd like to own books ourselves," he said. "But such a thing is difficult as long as we live with the banyan trees."

"Well, that's what we're here for. If you liked our services this time, please feel free to call upon us again. We'll always be there to deliver any book you want."

"Thank you. I mean it."

"Not at all. I'm more than happy to help with your daughter's present."

Kumu bowed his head profusely to me before going over to Ami. I watched him leave and sat down on a nearby large stump. All of a sudden, I was restless with the urge to see Shinonome-san. But I knew very well that I couldn't see him right that moment and tried to calm myself down. That was when Suimei approached.

"Chatting up the clients?" he asked.

"I certainly wouldn't phrase it that way..."

"What? Am I wrong?"

"No, I suppose not."

He sat down beside me and watched as Kuro ran like his life was on the line, fleeing from Nyaa-san, still holding that sea snake. I presumed Suimei had succeeded in getting the twins to eat the eyeballs in his stead. I watched his face in profile and, suddenly feeling emotional, loosened a worry I had been bottling. "Am I trying too hard?"

He didn't reply.

Even so, I continued. "Is it stupid of me to deliver books all the way out to the southern islands? I could have just used the time to take more shifts at my part-time job; that would have given me the money I need to pay for living expenses. If I wanted to bring more business to the bookstore, I could have just worked on advertising or something. But..."

I looked up at the fish wafting through the night air and felt like crying. "I want to deliver books to each and every spirit with a desire to read, as long as it's a distance my two feet can take me. That might make me a failure as a businesswoman, but if it means I can make even just one more spirit love books, I'm happy. Because I'm a book lover as well... I don't know, maybe I'm just being silly."

Suimei finally looked over at me and, with a soft smile and a chuckle, said, "I didn't say anything. You're just talking yourself down."

"Mgh... Wait, really?"

"Yup." He gazed up at the stars visible through the leaves of the banyan trees. "...Who cares?" he whispered. "Just do what you like."

He stood up and began to walk away.

"Suimei!" I rose to my feet and called after him. Taken at face value, his words were insincere. But I felt a deeper underlying meaning. "Do you really think it's okay for me to do what I want?" I asked.

He turned around and narrowed his eyes, brown and filled with sweetness, like bekkoame hard candy. "Yeah. I've seen you help many people firsthand just by delivering books."

Speaking no further, he left. Perhaps he meant to help Kinme and Ginme, currently being cornered by Nyaa-san.

I took a deep, long breath and placed my hand against my chest. My heart raced, badump-badump, as though cheering me on. "Yeah... I'll try my best!"

I psyched myself up and began my preparations for the night.

The moon had sunk a bit by the time the celebration reached its peak.

Everyone had begun presenting their presents to Ami. All around her, piles of beautiful seashell jewelry, brand-new leaf dresses, and fresh and dried fish towered higher and higher.

Ami, unable to speak, nodded deeply as she accepted every gift, then took the gifter's hands into her own and looked them in the eyes as she accepted their kind words. Then she stunned everyone with a smile so dazzling that even a human like me could understand that she was, indeed, the forest's most beautiful girl. Yet I couldn't help but feel conflicted every time I saw her smile; I felt like a faint shadow lay behind it.

Eventually, after the long line had dwindled and the majority of the presents had been given, Kumu came up to his daughter.

"Happy birthday, Ami."

She nodded deeply and smiled.

He smiled back, a bit bashfully. "I, um... I got you a present," he said hesitantly. "I hope you'll like it."

In his hands was a present enveloped in pink wrapping paper and gold-colored ribbon. The moment she laid eyes on this gift, so distinct from the rest, her face lit up. She excitedly began to undo the wrappings, taking diligent care not to damage whatever they might contain. It was as if she already knew whatever it was would be precious to her.

Inside were several picture books. Their covers alone showed a lot of thought had been put into their selection. They all contained excellent stories as well as wonderful illustrations, and they were appealing to children and adults alike.

Ami's eyes shot open wide the moment she saw the picture books, and she hugged them tightly against her chest. Pearl-like teardrops formed on her long eyelashes, and her cheeks flushed a rosy red. Her lovely face softened as a look of absolute, overwhelming joy took over.

"We're just borrowing the books, so we'll have to give them back eventually, but we can always borrow the ones you like again," Kumu said.

Ami nodded, looking over each picture book lovingly and tracing a finger over their covers. She came across one strange book that stood out from the rest, regarding it with some confusion before passing it over to her father.

"Hm? What's with this book? Did it get mixed in by accident?" he asked.

The book's cover and contents were completely blank. No matter how much he flipped through it, not a single illustration—let alone a word—was present. Deeply confused, the two looked at me.

I clenched my hands, clammy from my nerves, and smiled. "That book is a special magic book, one made by our very own bookstore. You need somebody who's been trained to read it... somebody like me, for example. Shall I read it for you? Everyone else is welcome to listen in, of course!"

The two looked at each other, then nodded.

*The real deal begins now. Let's do this!*

I psyched myself up and looked straight ahead.

Everyone gathered in front of the great banyan tree, sitting in a half-circle before me. I took a deep breath and, in a slightly theatrical tone, said, "My, oh my, what a strange item we have here. Could a blank book like this really be considered a book?"

Just then, Kuro came forward, holding a pail in his mouth. He strolled over, swinging his hips and wagging his tail, and placed the pail by my feet with a proud look on his face. I thanked him and plunged my hand into the pail.

"The truth is, this book changes with a little bit of magic. Here, let me show you..." I pulled a wet sponge out of the bucket and began to rub it against the book's cover.

"You'll soak the book!" somebody cried out. But their voice soon became a murmur of pleasant surprise, for the moment the sponge contacted the paper, the bright colors of an illustration began to reveal themselves.

This was a picture book with a twist. It was printed with a special ink that made the pictures appear only once the page had been wet.

I looked over everyone's faces, then began to give voice to the feelings stored within the book. "Once upon a time, there lived a happy father-daughter Kijimuna family."

Ami and Kumu looked at each other and smiled. They then looked back at the book, spellbound.

"The father, who lost his wife at a young age, and the daughter, who wanted to repay the father who worked hard to raise her alone—both wanted to do something for the other. Yet no matter how hard they thought, no good ideas came to mind. They lived in a forest, and in a forest, it was hard to come across special things. But that all changed one day when a certain man came to the forest."

I brushed the sponge against the page, revealing a gaudily dressed man wearing sunglasses.

"Tamaki-san...?" Recognizing the person pictured, the crowd began to whisper.

I grinned wryly to myself. Even in picture book form, Tamaki-san's unique style made him instantly recognizable. I continued the story. "The two Kijimuna each visited the man from the mainland, thinking he just might know what the perfect present would be. The first to visit was the father.

"The father spoke of his daughter's love for books, and the man agreed to provide some in exchange for something of value. And so, the father gave the man pearls he had painstakingly worked to collect. The man took the pearls and immediately chased the father away.

"The next day, the daughter visited the man and said she wanted to grant her father's dream."

"Huh? My dream?" Kumu mumbled, confused. Ami's naturally red face burned an even deeper shade of red as she hung her head.

"Upon hearing about the father's dream, the man boasted that he could grant it. He then demanded something of value in exchange, but unfortunately, the daughter had nothing to give.

'Very well, then,' the man said. 'Until your voice gives out, tell me everything you know.' The daughter did just that, teaching the man about the spirits of Okinawa, of the folktales of every region, and of the stories passed orally through generations of Kijimuna. She continued for three days and three nights, until her voice grew hoarse and vanished. The man, satisfied, left."

I only got that far when Kumu interrupted me in a fit of pique. He grabbed Ami's arm and bellowed, "I thought you lost your voice to a cold! Oh, no... How could such a thing happen to your lovely voice?!"

Ami slipped out of his grasp and shook her head with a smile. She then looked over at me and nodded deeply.

I was left momentarily stunned by Kumu's outburst, but I regained my composure and continued, brushing a page with the sponge. The image of the daughter, praying, appeared.

"The daughter prayed every day for her wish to be granted. But no matter how many days passed, the man never returned. She began to wonder if she was tricked when, right on her birthday, a group of people arrived with books."

Just then, Kinme and Ginme approached from behind. The two hefted over a large cooler box we had brought from the spirit realm and set it down.

"The group delivered the books to the father. With this, he now had a present to give to his daughter for her birthday. The father's request had been granted...and now the daughter's could be too."

Ami took her father's hands into hers. Her eyes were wet with tears as she looked at her father, who stared back at her in confusion.

In her place, I said, "Kumu-san, I hear you have a dream. Would you be so kind as to tell everyone here what it is?"

Overcome with emotion, Kumu couldn't find the right words. We all patiently waited, until finally, he began to speak. "...Ever... ever since I was a young boy, I've wanted to see snow!"

I smiled as I wet the next page with the sponge, revealing a banyan tree blanketed in pure-white snow. "Then allow us to grant your wish!"

Kinme and Ginme threw open the cooler box. From inside blew a gust of frigid air.

Large snowflakes gracefully fluttered down into the forest. It was now cold enough for our breath to be visible, and the vibrant deep green that was characteristic of the tropics was dyed white, bit by bit. Snow drifted through the air and showed no signs of stopping, and something flew as well—not fish, but a group of women clad in white. Yuki-Onna.

"Whooooaaa! It's snowing!" the Kijimuna exclaimed. They gleefully grabbed at the snow in the air and built snowmen from the thin layer that formed on the ground. Kuro and Nyaa-san, as well as Kinme and Ginme, joined them, quickly becoming covered in snow. No matter their age, each and every one of them played to their heart's content in the pure-white dreamscape.

"In truth, it snowed here in Okinawa once, a few years ago," Kumu admitted bashfully. His face beamed as he watched the snow. "But I was asleep then and missed it. I only learned how wonderful it was from everyone afterward. I was so distraught to have slept through a chance to fulfill my dream. To think you remembered..."

Kumu put his hands on Ami's cheeks, tears streaming from his eyes. "Thank you for granting my dream, but you shouldn't have traded your voice for it. My dream is nothing next to your lovely voice..."

He hugged her, tears still streaming down. Ami blinked a few times, seemingly confused.

"Pfft!" I couldn't help but laugh.

Suimei, standing next to me, shot me a nasty glare. "There's nothing funny about this. She lost her voice!"

"Pft, ha ha ha... B-but—" I wiped the tears out of my eyes and said, "Tamaki-san doesn't have the ability to steal somebody's voice or anything."

"Huh?"

"Ami's voice is just worn out. That's all."

As I said that, a Yuki-Onna approached, descending before Ami. She took out something from her breast pocket and said with a laugh, "Did you know pearls are also known as mermaid tears? The same mermaids who sing such lovely songs."

In her hand was a large pearl. The moment he saw it, Kumu exclaimed, "That's my pearl!"

The Yuki-Onna pulled out yet another object from her breast pocket, this time a packet of powdered medicine. She opened the packet, crushed the pearl between her fingers, and mixed the two before handing it to Ami. "This is a special medicine made by an apothecary in the spirit realm. Go ahead, swallow it down. All spirits who sing make frequent use of this medicine."

Ami nodded, and she nervously swallowed down the medicine. She tried to speak, but her throat could only make a wheezing sound. Kumu slumped his shoulders, looking like all hope was lost, until...

"Aaah... Aah!"

"Ami?!"

"Aaah, I can speak. I can speak!" she exclaimed, her voice as clear and beautiful as the ringing of a bell. She hugged her father, overjoyed.

Kumu's face wrinkled into a smile. "Amazing. Today's supposed to be Ami's birthday, and yet it feels like it's mine at the same time."

Pearl-like tears fell down his cheeks as he gently hugged his daughter back.

"So that's why you went out of your way to go through the Hell of the Crimson Lotus?" Suimei asked me as Ami consoled her weeping father.

"Heh heh. Whatever are you talking about?" I replied. He was right on the money, of course. We had picked up the Yuki-Onna when we passed through that very hell. They had been more than happy to come along when presented with those pearls.

"You even prepared some medicine from Noname and that picture book. Pretty thorough."

"Heh, I had a lot of help. But feel free to compliment me more, if you'd like."

The blank book I'd read today was, of course, durable against water. I intended to give it to the father-daughter pair as a present, rather than the rest, which we were just lending. The pictures were a bit amateurish, but...I thought it'd still make a nice gift.

"Just who was the guy who arranged this order anyway? Another philanthropist like you?"

"Well...not exactly." I reached out and let a piece of snow fall into my hand. "A man named Tamaki-san helped set this up, but he's not exactly as kind as you think."

"What do you mean?"

I handed Suimei the order form I'd received from Tamaki-san. On it were various details ranging from how to call out the Kijimuna, Kumu's dream, Ami's love for books, and her birthday... but that was all. There wasn't a single mention or suggestion on what to do, just plain facts listed out.

"This is normal for him. He leaves me with only the information and forces me to figure out what to do with it, basically saying, 'Whether you succeed or not depends on you alone.'"

"Then what would have happened if things hadn't played out like they did? What if you screwed up and let down your customers?"

"I'd imagine he'd say the fault lay with me alone. I had all the information I needed but failed to make proper use of it." I shrugged, then thought back on that weirdly dressed friend of my adoptive father's. "That's just how he is. He'll get you the necessary info but won't tell what path you need to go down. Even if you wind up taking the wrong route, he still won't say a thing.

It's like he's the character in a story who tells the main character where to go without caring what dangers they might face."

"What the heck?" Suimei grimaced.

It certainly did sound like Tamaki-san was irresponsible for not caring what came of things, but in a way, he could also have been considered kind for trusting in my ability to work things out.

"I don't know why he chooses to do things like this, but it's how he is. He urges others to move but only observes the result from afar himself. It's like he only cares about watching how things develop." I sighed. My white breath quickly faded into the air. "The fact that I can't understand him sometimes frightens me...but he can't be all that bad if he's Shinonome-san's friend."

"You certainly trust Shinonome a lot..."

"Of course I do. He's my father!"

Suimei let out a deep sigh and bonked me on the head. "So the delivering of books, making a performance out of the picture book, and the snow were all your idea? You're a real softie. Jeez..." With some exasperation, he added, "You'd really do anything to help others, huh?"

"Should I not?" I asked, smiling impishly.

He shrugged back and began, "Just do—" but stopped mid-sentence and thought some. The corners of his mouth turned upward in a faint smile. "Nah. It's very much like you."

"Hee hee, thank you."

Once again, I looked back to the clearing. Bit by bit, the subtropical forest grew whiter before my eyes. The Kijimuna frolicked, enjoying the once-in-a-lifetime moment to the fullest with bright smiles on their faces. Those smiles were thanks to us, and thanks to a single book we had brought along.

"I'm glad I brought that book after all..."

With this, all my hard work was repaid in full.

I smiled, then put my hand over my warm chest.

Some time later, while we were undergoing preparations to make our way home, Ami approached. Kumu had drunk himself to sleep by this point after celebrating on awamori, a strong Okinawan liquor.

Ami gazed at her father, loudly snoring to the side. "Thank you for today," she said. "I've always wanted to repay my father before I became married."

"Like father, like daughter, I guess..." I said, eliciting a confused look from her. I proceeded to tell her what her father had said earlier: *As a father, I wanted to do something for Ami; I wanted to give her a memory she would never forget even after she married.*

Tears streamed down her face as she smiled. "I swear...I'll always love my father. I won't leave him all by himself, even after I get married."

I offered her a handkerchief with a smile. Tears fell, but from a place of happiness. I squinted, finding myself a little envious. As blood-related family, those two could unconditionally love each other.

*How nice. A fake daughter like me could never be like that...*

I knew there was nothing I could do about it, but the realization still hurt from time to time.

"Is something the matter?" Ami asked.

"No, nothing." I extended a hand to her. "If you ever feel like reading, please, order from us again."

With a beaming smile, she nodded. "Of course! I'll do just that."

I smiled as well, nodding back. "Let the haunted bookstore take care of all your bookish needs!"

# CHAPTER 2

# The Great Tengu of Mount Kurama

THE SKY OF THE SPIRIT REALM changed to a vibrant maroon purple.

At long last, autumn had come to the world of perpetual night. Autumn was the season when crops became ripe. It was also the season when preparations for winter began.

Once the mountains took on warmer autumn colors, carts full of vegetables and grains harvested from every corner of the spirit realm would flock to town. The sight of these travelers, lit by glimmerflies caged in lanterns affixed to the edge of carts and to large knapsacks, was iconic enough to be considered characteristic of the season itself.

Vendors on the main street switched out their usual wares for ones meant to fight the winter cold. Hawkers walked about with buckets of vegetables attached to a pole slung over their shoulders, searching for buyers. A number of stalls set up shop along the roadside, filling the main street with a motley spread of items.

A large fish swayed in the air, tied up and slung across the back of a spirit carrying a bale of salt.

The kappa, the baka-danuki, the oni, even the ochimusha—absolutely everyone busied themselves with winter preparations. The echoing din of people haggling over goods, while not quite comparable to the bustle of summer festivals, was indicative of a strong, healthy economy.

Dried vegetables and fish hung from the eaves of buildings, every free inch and moment dedicated to the coming winter. Yet everyone moved about with cheery expressions. The joy of harvest, the delicacies of autumn, the comfortable and gentle climate—all those pleasures showed on their faces.

Summer was special, that I cannot deny. But autumn, too, was special in its own way. Its world of warm colors gave us a moment's respite before the harsh season that followed.

As the spirits busied themselves with winter preparations, our store readied itself for its own annual event.

"Whew, there we go." I carried a stack of books over to a rush mat laid out in front of the store. I say books, but that really meant all kinds of things: paperbacks, hardcovers, magazines, encyclopedias, you name it. Carefully, I lined them up on the mat. I took in the view and keenly felt that autumn had, indeed, arrived.

Just then, the young neighboring housewife (an Oni who had married two hundred years ago, if that's still considered young) happened to be walking by and called out to me. "Oh, Kaori-chan.

Getting ready to air out the books? You're sure getting a good sweat in."

"Ha ha, yeah. It's a real hassle every year with how much we have to go through."

"Well, why don't I bring over some persimmons later? Enough for everyone."

"Really? That'd be great!"

I watched as she entered her house, then wiped the sweat off my brow. The wind was cool and pleasant now that it was autumn. I felt a bit emotional at the fact that I could wipe sweat away and not still feel sticky all over, unlike in the humid summer. It might have just been my imagination, but the glimmerflies felt more energetic than usual, as though they were overjoyed to be free of the summer heat as well.

Suimei appeared, holding books in his arms.

"Where do you want these?" he said gruffly.

"O-oh, there please. Sorry, are they heavy?"

"It's fine." He nodded, obediently carried the books to where I indicated, and then made for the store again. That was when I realized he wasn't joined by that usual little bundle of energy.

"Where's Kuro?" I asked.

Suimei made a face like his heart had been torn in two and looked toward the back of the store. "He's...not feeling so great right now."

Shocked, I followed his gaze and saw a black lump lying in a corner. It was Kuro, quietly whining like he was in pain. His long body was limply curled into the shape of a bagel, and his breaths were shallow.

"Is he okay?" I asked.

"Totally fine. He just ate too much because it's autumn. I already gave him some medicine."

"O-oh." *Well that's...a bit lame for an Inugami.*

I took another look at Kuro. Not too long ago, he and Suimei had worked as exorcists to hunt down spirits. Not a trace of that former life could be seen now, however. Kuro would probably deny it himself, but he honestly acted just like any other ordinary dog.

Suimei grinned wryly and shrugged. "It seems life's been nothing but fun for him lately. Maybe a bit too fun." His eyes softened some, and he continued with a gentle tone. "Maybe it's because he doesn't have to hurt anyone anymore... Which is a good thing, I guess."

As exorcists, their days had been spent chasing spirits. The peace they had now was still somewhat new to them. New enough to, say, get carried away and end up with a tummy ache.

I smiled, finding myself agreeing with Suimei's words. "Are you not going to look after him?"

"He'll be fine. And this is just me repaying what I owe you. Don't worry about it." With that, he went inside to get more books.

"Awoo!"

I heard Kuro yelp and worriedly looked over. Standing atop him was Nyaa-san, walking all over him like it were her god-given right.

"Nyaa..." I began to say something out of worry for Kuro, but the sight was so strange that I just shut my mouth instead.

"What? Are you not going to run away today?" Nyaa-san spat with a hint of disappointment, before sitting down and curling up into a ball right on top of Kuro. She often tormented him by chasing him around, amongst other things, but I knew deep down that she cared for him.

The sourpuss of a black cat let out a tremendous yawn and closed her eyes. Her three tails swayed above Kuro's body as though she was petting him.

*Oh, Nyaa-san...*

As a faint smile rose to my lips, I spun one of my tired, heavy arms in a circle. My arms were spent from carrying books all morning. Our goal for the day was to get out all the books on the bottom row of the first floor's shelves, but...could we really manage it?

Still a bit worried, I followed Suimei into the store.

For bookstores, autumn was the season for airing out books.

If left alone too long, books could become infested with insects. One such book-infecting insect is the silverfish, perhaps better known as the bookworm; they eat the glue and the paper in books for their starch. Older books are at a higher risk of infestation, so our bookstore had a particular need to air out our wares.

We also took the opportunity to clean the shop and do any maintenance on books that needed it, so things got pretty busy. We had to brush away all the dust, wipe all the dirty book covers, and set aside any books in need of repairs. All in all, everything usually took around a whole month.

"Whew... Finally done." I let out a tired sigh. It had taken a few hours, but we had finally managed to set out all the bottom row books on the first floor.

I pulled out a nearby chair, sat in it, and looked inside the store, feeling impressed yet again by just how many books there were. Our home was a two-story wooden building that looked a bit older than the surrounding structures. The bookstore portion took up part of the first floor and didn't look that big from the outside, but everything changed once you went in. Bookshelves that stretched so high, their tops couldn't be seen lined the walls of the small shop, which was only sixteen meters square. Each shelf was crammed with books Shinonome-san had spent many, many hours collecting.

The only lighting inside was the dim light of hanging glimmerfly lamps that swayed with every beat of glimmerfly wings. Installed against the endlessly continuing bookshelves were several time-worn, pockmarked ladders that allowed access to the books higher up.

*Ah... That brings back memories.* I looked at the ladders and affectionately thought back to my childhood. Those ladders had instilled such wonder in me then. I'd thought an adventure like the ones I had read of in books awaited me at the top, so I secretly climbed them together with young Kinme and Ginme countless times. Those grand adventures had always ended in Shinonome-san's scolding, however.

I smiled at the memory and began wiping the now empty shelves.

There were many strange things about this bookstore. The unnaturally tall bookshelves never filled up no matter how many books were placed on their shelves. The shelves on the ground could be moved, revealing more shelves behind them, or even, if moved in a certain order, a set of stairs leading to a basement.

The well-hidden basement was for Shinonome-san's exclusive use and kept off limits to everyone, including me. At this point, I figured it probably contained a library of valuable books that needed to be kept away from clumsy hands, but the younger me hadn't thought the same.

I mean, it was a secret room nobody was allowed to enter. It had practically begged to be explored by a younger Kaori.

I hadn't snuck in lately, being an adult, but when I was a kid, I'd gone all the time with Nyaa-san whenever Shinonome-san wasn't around.

*I wonder if that's still there...* A thought crossed my mind, and I began to walk. Shinonome-san was out of the house today...so surely it'd be all right if I took a small peek inside?

"Oooh..." I moved the bookshelves and peered down into the basement. There were lamps, but they lacked glimmerflies, so it was dark. I could barely make out a wooden shelf filled with scrolls and other ancient-looking books occupying the small room.

The curious spirit of my youth seemed to make a resurgence. *...Should I go in?*

"What're you slacking off for?"

"Eeek!" My heart leapt out my chest, and I quickly turned around. Standing there was a displeased-looking Suimei. *Oh, shoot!*

My mind immediately tried to come up with an excuse, but I soon realized there was an even better option. I could make him my co-conspirator.

"Hello there, young man. Say, how about you and I go on a little adventure?" Smiling, I grabbed a nearby lamp and hugged one of his arms.

He gave me a weary frown. "Don't be stupid. We still have so much—"

"Ha ha ha, what're you saying, young'un?" I interrupted and began pulling him toward the basement. "If now's not the time for adventure, when will it be?"

"You're only three years older than me..." He resisted some, a frown still on his face, but he quickly relented and descended with me.

It was chilly at the bottom of the stairs. The air was humid and slightly tinged with the scent of mold. Melted wax adhered to the bottom of a candle stand attached to the stone wall. On the ceiling, I could see a small spider on a web.

"So, what's this place then?" Suimei asked.

"It's where rare books and really old documents are kept," I answered. "There's even some things here that aren't in the human world. It's usually off limits to anyone other than Shinonome-san, but there's something weird in the back I wanted to see."

"Something weird...?"

I moved quietly, making sure my footsteps made no sound, and proceeded farther into the basement. I reached the back in no time at all, as it really wasn't that big.

"I-It's still here..." Before me was a door sealed by countless talismans. The door was coated in red paint, and the talismans had some incomprehensible spell written on them in yellow ink. I'd known about the door since I was a child, but I'd never once seen what was beyond it.

"I've always wanted to know what was past this thing," I said while staring at the mysterious door.

"What's this?" Suimei asked, his curiosity piqued by the talismans despite being so against coming down just moments prior. "I don't think I've seen these kinds of talismans before. They're clearly meant to seal away something... Is this Chinese? At the very least, it's obvious these weren't placed recently. I can tell they're strong too; there's no way weak spirits could approach this."

"Is it really that strong?"

"Yeah. There's not much effect on humans, but it'd repel most spirits. What's something like this doing in the basement of a bookstore?"

Even Suimei, a former exorcist, was stumped. I was beginning to get suspicious.

"Just what could you have that you'd hide from everyone, even your own adoptive daughter?" I wondered out loud.

"Dunno."

It had to be something important to be worth putting sturdy seals upon. Unless...

"If it's his porn or something, I'd really rather not know..."
I said.

"Kaori? What're you doing here?"

"Eeek!"

Just then, a voice—one a bit deep for a woman yet still dripping with allure—called out, making me jump. I timidly looked back at the entrance of the basement to see Noname, the spirit who'd raised me in place of a mother, standing there.

"We've told you many times not to enter that room, haven't we?"

"I'm sorry..." What had a twenty-year-old woman like me been thinking, anyway?

We had left the basement and moved to the living room. I slumped my shoulders, ashamed for acting like a child.

Noname squinted her amber eyes and giggled. "I'm not mad, dear. But you should really get Shinonome's permission before you go down there."

"Noname..." I was moved to tears by her sweetness.

"More importantly, that young housewife from next door brought over some persimmons. I peeled them for you, so eat up."

"Oh, they look delicious." I bounced back in an instant and cheerfully sat down at the low table. The ripe persimmons oozed juices when pierced with a fork. I put a piece in my mouth and let the sweetness wash away my fatigue. Despite being fruits, they were as sweet as desserts. They were soft enough to practically melt away in my mouth as I bit into them, sliding down my throat with ease.

"It's really autumn…" That flavor definitely drove home the fact that autumn had arrived. I felt so happy that I thought I might just melt away together with the persimmons.

That was when Suimei, sitting next to me and also eating, mumbled out, "So, what's next? We brought the books outside, but…aren't you usually supposed to air them out under the sun?"

He looked out the window. The sky of the spirit realm was perfectly clear, the stars beaming beautifully. But there was no sunlight to be had in this world of perpetual night, so airing out the books would do nothing to rid them of any pests they might have between their pages.

The solution was simple: bring them to a sunny place.

"It's fine, it's fine," I said. "Those books will—"

"Be taken to our place," a familiar voice suddenly said. I turned around to face the source.

"Are those persimmons? Gimme some too!"

"Hello, everyone. Ginme, where's your greeting?"

The Raven Tengu twins Kinme and Ginme had arrived.

Amongst all Tengu legends across Japan, there was one location more famous than any other—Mount Kurama, located in Kyoto Prefecture and a former site of ascetic Buddhist training.

There exists a theory that in the olden days, the mountain was called Mount Kurabu, meaning "dark place." Sure enough, the forest of cedar and cypress covering the mountain didn't leave much room for light. The lack of broadleaf trees also meant autumn didn't bring about much change of color; the vigorous hue of the evergreen trees blanketed the mountainsides year-round. This gave the area an air of solemnity, one that lived up to its reputation as a sacred mountain.

The famous Minamoto no Yoshitsune was said to have learned swordsmanship there from Kurama Sojobo, the Great Tengu of Kurama. A giant Tengu face was installed in front of Eizan Electric Railway's Kurama Station to pay homage to the mountain's Tengu legend.

It was a mountain visited by many people, and yet it remained a headquarters for the Tengu. That included the Raven Tengu Kinme and Ginme as well.

"We're home, Gramps!"

"We've returned, Sojobo-sama."

"Mm-hmm. Welcome back."

Halfway up the mountain, hidden by a forest of cedars, was the desolate ruins of a temple. This was where the twins made their home in the human world. They didn't live here alone but with the man awaiting our arrival from atop a broken stone lantern—Kurama Sojobo. He looked exactly how one would expect a Tengu to look, having a red face and a long nose over a mustache. He wore a monk's robe with a black base that had golden-yellow puffs on it. On his forehead was the sort of small cap that mountain ascetics wore, and on his feet were long, lacquered wooden geta.

Sojobo was a powerful Tengu who lived on Mount Kurama and was one of the forty-eight great Tengu of Japan listed in the secret Tengu-Kyo Buddhist prayer sutra. He was also a regular of our bookstore and the spirit who looked after the twin baby birds I'd found when I was five, Kinme and Ginme.

This abandoned temple was where our bookstore would do its airing out. We needed a slightly dim place like this, as strong sunlight could cause the colors of the book covers to fade. The temple grounds were also just the right size to spread out the entirety of our collection, so Sojobo let us use the place every year. I should also mention that hauling the books back was a challenge in its own right, so we planned to stay the night there.

"Thank you for letting us use your temple again this year, Sojobo-sama."

"Is that you, Kaori? Well now, you've grown into a splendid young woman."

"Really? Ehe heh..."

"If your breasts and ass grew just a bit more, you'd be perfect."

"You gotta be kidding me." I gave him a nasty look, to which he laughed heartily. The way he acted like an insensitive old man at times was just so annoying.

"Wow, your hair's all white!" a cute voice said.

"Are you a white bird, Mister?" another asked.

"I'm not a white bird."

"Then what bird are you?" the two voices chorused.

"I'm not a bird."

A pair of twin boys, somewhere around three years old, gazed up at Suimei with eyes full of wonder. They looked like miniature versions of Kinme and Ginme. Suimei seemed unsure of how to deal with small children and kept his answers brief. That was when Kinme and Ginme noticed the two and called out to them.

"Oh, Sora, Umi! Were you waiting for us too?" Ginme asked.

"Hello, there. Want me to carry you in my arms?" Kinme offered.

"Kin-chan, Gin-chan!" The children beamed as they hugged the older twins. They wrapped their small hands around Ginme's and Kinme's neck and affectionately pressed their cheeks against theirs. "Welcome home!"

Sora and Umi were Raven Tengu being raised by Sojobo. In a sense, they were Kinme and Ginme's younger pupils under the same master, as even at their young age, they were undergoing daily training to become upstanding Tengu.

"Kao-chan, welcome! Is it time to air out the books?"

"We'll help!"

The twins' pudgy cheeks tinted red as they happily offered their help. When I accepted it, they giggled with their small toddler hands over their mouths.

"Gramps says he'll give us mochi if we do a good job."

"Mochi is yummy! You should eat some too, Kao-chan."

So the snacks were what they were really after... Regardless, having such cute helpers made me smile. "Mochi sounds nice; I'm looking forward to it. Shall we begin?"

"Yeah!" they declared.

I rolled up my sleeves and psyched myself up.

"Wait." But Suimei immediately put a damper on things.

"What's up?"

"Well..." He frowned, then pointed ahead. "How exactly are you going to air out your books with all that?"

"Oh..." I looked to where he pointed and saw the temple grounds were overgrown with weeds. A bit of the stone paving could be faintly seen peeking out from under it, but most of the stone was hidden underneath the greenery. It looked like one of those empty lots for sale that no one had been looking after and was clearly not ready for the books.

Sojobo let out a hearty laugh. "Sorry, Kaori! I told Kinme and Ginme to weed the place by today, but it looks like something came up!" He shot a sharp look toward the twins and in a low voice said, "Care to explain, boys?"

The two paled and ran to Suimei.

"I-It's okay, Gramps! We'll do it right away!"

"We weren't slacking off; we just never found the right time to get to it... But Suimei's here today, so we can get it done super fast."

"What—hey! What's the meaning of this?" Suimei complained.

"You'll help us, right, Suimei? We're friends, right?!" The twins pleaded with Suimei, their eyes moist.

Suimei seemed reluctant for a moment, but he soon let out a defeated sigh. "...Fine."

"Awww yeah, I knew you would help us, Suimei! You're a man among men, nothing like that old fart!"

"Thank you, Suimei. I'm less scared of that monster of a grandfather with you here."

"Did you say something, you brats?" Sojobo said.

The twins quickly straightened their backs and shouted, "Nope, not a thing!" before scurrying over to the overgrown temple grounds.

"Those two sure get along well," I commented.

"As idiots tend to do."

Sojobo and I shared a look and smiled. I then began getting the books ready for airing out.

The process for airing out books was simple. You first put on some gloves and flipped through the pages wildly to make sure any bugs fell out. Then you stood the book up vertically, leaving it open slightly so the wind could breeze through it. Finally, you let it stay like that for a while.

Humidity was the mortal enemy of books. Mold damaged every part of them and even coaxed bugs into pages. We tried to take measures against mold, but in a world of perpetual darkness, humidity was unavoidable. That was why we had to air out the books every year. It was difficult with so many to go through, but I was ready to do anything for the precious books we lent to our customers.

I set about my work on the areas that had been weeded.

Some time passed, and the trees rustled as the wind swept through them. Suimei silently plucked the weeds, before abruptly shouting, "There's just no end to these things!"

He sat down and looked up at the sky. The autumn sky of the human world was perfectly clear. The cheeps of a small bird could be heard. The humidity was low enough to make one want to take a nap. Sadly, none of those things made the endless weeding any less tiresome. He flopped onto his back.

"You all right?" I asked, sitting next to him with a thermos and a towel. Inside the thermos was cold tea with a bit of honey mixed in for sweetness.

He sat himself up, took the thermos, and drank vigorously from it. With a bit of bitterness, he looked over at Sojobo. "Can't you use some Tengu ability to weed the place in seconds?"

"Ba ha ha! This is training, sonny. Training for your endurance, grip strength, and concentration."

"I don't need any such training. I'm an apothecary."

Sojobo smiled boldly. "Whether you're an apothecary or an *exorcist*, endurance and concentration are both important, no?"

Suimei's expression turned grim. He clearly hadn't expected Sojobo to know about his exorcist past. His expression soon softened though, once the voices of the older twins noisily weeding beside Umi and Sora drifted toward us. "...Right," Suimei murmured. "You're their master."

"Those two report everything back to me, so naturally, I've heard a great deal about you!"

Suimei sighed and gazed out at the temple grounds, still overrun with weeds. "This place is a mess. Those fancy temples elsewhere on the mountain draw in tourists looking for Tengu, right? Why not put some effort in and do the same?"

Sojobo let out another hearty laugh—before abruptly turning stony-faced. "Well... This place is in such a mess because humans have decided we spirits don't exist."

Confused, Suimei met his eyes. Sojobo gave him a wide, toothy grin before continuing. "Hear me out now. There probably aren't many in Japan who don't know what spirits are. We've been by each other's sides for all these years, after all."

"Spirits do often appear in anime and manga, yeah," Suimei said.

"Right," I agreed. "The more famous spirits are recognizable to children and adults alike."

"That's the kind of stuff that *killed* us," Sojobo said, pointing at us two. "Not just those anime and manga things, but those books you're working so hard to air out as well. Even that TV whatnot."

"Huh...?" I was speechless.

He continued without pause. "We spirits used to live in the gaps of reality and imagination. We existed to those who believed we did, and we didn't to those who didn't believe."

I didn't know what to do with that word, "exist." Did spirits qualify? Maybe they did—but spirits had a kind of vague existence.

The people of long, long ago had felt presences in the darkness beyond. They attributed sounds they couldn't place and phenomena they couldn't understand to those presences. But with the advent of media and science, spirits had been declared nonexistent. The darkness they dwelled in was cleared away, and they were dragged into the world of light.

"Humans declared us creations, products of the imagination, unrealistic, things that never existed from the start. That thing called, er...science? It cleared away any mysteries surrounding us. In the past, we lived together with those who believed we existed.

They would have cleaned these grounds up right away, and we'd have repaid them in kind. Things were fun back then..." Sojobo said with a sad smile. "But those times are over now. The ones who truly believed we existed are gone, and most of the spirits that lived in the human world have moved to the spirit realm. It's a bit sad, but really, what's so unusual about the relics of the past being weeded away?"

Books had killed the spirits of the human world. The same books I loved so dearly.

I looked down at the books that were airing out. Most were fiction stories, many featuring spirits. I had been oh so happy to read them, even thrilled to see spirits I knew appear within them. But those same stories were the very reason they had lost their place in the world...

I paled. My body began to chill, starting from my extremities, and it became difficult for me to even stand.

That was when Sojobo grinned wryly. "It ain't anything you need to feel bad about, Kaori. It's just nature running its course. The world changes. It's not anybody's fault. Not even the books." He scratched his beard, still reminiscing. "Come to think of it, I had this conversation with someone else recently... I think it was with...Shinonome?"

"Huh? With Shinonome-san?" I said, surprised. That was the last name I'd expected to hear.

Sojobo smacked his fist against his palm. "Oh, that's right, that's right. Said he was collecting data, he did. Asked me a bunch of weird questions too."

"Oh really?"

"Anyway, you needn't feel bad about anything. It's not like you directly caused this yourself." He tousled my hair with his large hands and laughed heartily. "Besides, it's not like it really matters if humans stop believing in us. Sure, I'm a bit sad I won't be able to meet an interesting fellow like Yoshitsune again, but at the end of the day, humans and spirits have always been separate. We just happened to be sharing the same space for a while, that's all."

*But that's...so sad.* I averted my gaze from Sojobo's smile and clenched my fist.

We succeeded in airing out all the books we brought that day. We then gathered them up and bundled them together. Now all we had to do was wait for Nyaa-san to come pick us up the next day.

Evening neared. The distant sky began to take on a rose madder-red glow as birds returned to their beds and chirped from nearby. As one would expect, weeding the grounds of an entire temple was exhausting. Suimei was fast asleep on the abandoned temple's open veranda, and I sat next to him, vacantly watching the clouds drift across the sky.

"Yo, Kaori!"

"Kao-chan, you finished!"

Ginme and Sora appeared. Ginme had done the same weeding work as Suimei but was still somehow full of life. He was even giving Sora a ride on his shoulders. Perhaps it was because of his daily training that he still had so much energy. He sat down next to me and peered at me with his cheery eyes. "Ready for some-thing nice?"

"Huh?"

"Heh heh... Sora."

"Here you go, Kao-chan!" Sora pulled out a Japanese sweet. I beamed with delight the instant I saw it, for it was nothing other than my favorite sweet in the whole wide world.

"For me?" I asked.

"Yup. You worked hard today, right? Let's eat it together." Ginme scanned the area and double-checked Suimei was asleep before bringing his pointer finger to his lips and saying, "Let's keep this a secret between us, though. There ain't any for Suimei."

"Ha ha, all right. I'm surprised you managed to get your hands on these," I said.

He had brought a set of mochi that was anecdotally associated with Minamoto no Yoshitsune, a famous historical figure who had lived on Mount Kurama for a time. They could only be bought at the confectionery in front of the Kurama Temple gate and were filled with chestnuts and sweet bean paste. The mochi was stretchy, and the sweet bean paste was strained and well-salted, making for the perfect treat. Not too sweet and just the right size. The product was popular enough to be sold out before noon on some days.

"Gin-chan woke up super early to get these because you were coming today! Even though he's always sleeping in!" Sora proudly shared.

"Wha—Sora?! I said don't tell her! Here, this one's yours. Now leave."

"Yaaay! Sweets!" Sora accepted his piece and trotted off, his feet going pitter-patter against the wood.

Ginme averted his gaze out of embarrassment. I thanked him, causing his cheeks to flush red. "It's whatever," he curtly replied.

"Mmm! So good! These are perfect after a day's work..."

"Right? Man, I shoulda bought more..."

The two of us tore through the mochi in no time and were left with a sad, empty container. My throat felt a bit dry, so I poured us some tea out of the thermos.

"Thanks, Kaori. Oh, this is good."

"Isn't it? This be some of our finest, my dear sir."

"Nothing strange mixed in, is there...?"

"I make no promises!"

The two of us joked around and laughed like we always did.

Then, out of the blue, Ginme looked truly relieved. "Thank goodness. I was worried that earlier stuff was weighing on your mind."

"Oh..." In an instant, Sojobo's words returned to me and my mood crumbled. I shut my eyes tight, trying not to cry.

Ginme grew flustered. "Whoa, uh, did I make you remember?! My bad... Dang! Why am I always like this?!" He roughly rubbed my head, making a mess of my hair.

"Stop it! You're messing up my hair!"

"Huh? Oh... Was that too strong? Weird... You also chin up when Shinonome does it."

"What are you talking about? Maybe when I was a child, sure."

"Hmm... Really?"

I couldn't help but smile at how awkwardly Ginme was trying to cheer me up. He smiled too, a bit abashed. He had succeeded some.

"Thank you. I feel a bit better now," I said.

"...That's good."

I looked up at the rose madder sky and gradually began to open up. "Maybe what I'm doing is horrible, lending spirits the very things that are harming them. Or maybe Sojobo is right, and I shouldn't worry about it... I don't know."

Ginme frowned. "I was listening earlier, but... Well, to be honest, I don't really get that kind of complicated stuff one bit. But I do know the only ones who care about those kinds of things are people like Gramps and Shinonome; most spirits don't think about that kind of stuff at all."

"Really?"

"Yeah. Why else would they be borrowing books in the first place?"

"But..." Sojobo's words made sense. I'd noticed myself that the number of spirits living in the human world was decreasing. The gap between the two worlds was widening.

Ginme suddenly smacked his fist against his palm. "I got it!" He looked at me and said, "Make sure you're free tonight. Oh, and let's get Nyaa in on this too. This is going to be good!"

"What?" I asked, bewildered.

Ginme gave me the most refreshing smile. "I got something nice to show you!"

"Think you could give some notice next time, instead of waiting until the last moment to invite me?" Nyaa-san asked.

"Oh, don't be like that," I replied. "Ginme says he has something nice to show us!"

"I had plans to sleep all day."

"I said I was sorry!"

Suimei, a disgruntled Nyaa-san, and I met up and went to the cedar tree Ginme had told me that he would be waiting at. Our surroundings had just begun to darken, as it was around six in the evening.

Once we met him, Ginme led us to a certain place.

"W-wait, should we be doing this?!" I asked.

"It'll be fine! The humans won't see us!" he reassured me.

"A-are you sure?!"

Ginme descended the mountain at an alarming speed, running across treetops and temple roofs with deft steps, just barely out of sight of the temple-goers offering worship. On his back was me, utterly floored by his speed.

"You better not drop Kaori, Ginme!" Nyaa-san, following shortly behind us, shot a sharp glare at him. He had offered to carry me in place of her today, saying he had someplace he wanted to show me personally.

Ginme looked back at her and nodded deeply, then, with a little worry in his voice, said, "I know! You should be more worried about Suimei—he's about to fall off!"

"It's fine. He's a former exorcist; he'll manage even if he falls," she replied.

"I-It's not f-f-fine at all!" Suimei cried, hanging on for dear life to Nyaa-san's back. She showed no care whatsoever for this particular rider. *Perhaps only I got special treatment?*

"What'd I tell you? You should have let me carry you," said Kinme.

"No, let us carry the white one!" Sora said.

"That sounds fun! We can zip and whoosh through the air together!" Umi said.

"Ab-so-*lutely* not!" Suimei fiercely shook his head as he turned down their offers. *Maybe it was something to do with his pride as a man? ...Well, I would also have refused the two small ones, if I were being honest.*

After some more back and forth, we eventually reached our destination: a village at the base of the mountain, sandwiched between Mount Kurama and the Kurama River. Many ancient buildings that looked full of history stood in rows, proof that the street they were on had once flourished with activity. It had been one of ancient Japan's numbered highways, connecting the former provinces of Tanba and Wakasa. Ginme stopped on the roof of one building, let me down, and began surveying the area. I surveyed it as well, checking out just where he'd brought me to.

"There's a lot of people for some reason," I commented.

"Wonder why," Nyaa-san mused, having landed behind me.

The sky there was already beginning to dim, yet locals and tourists filled the streets, moving to and fro. When I looked at the second-floor windows of shops and ryokan inns, I saw hordes of people clustered against them. Everyone eagerly awaited something. Even though it was night, nobody made any efforts to leave—far from it, more and more people appeared as I watched.

What was more, a strange object was placed here and there along the line of buildings. It looked like a club made out of bundled wood, and it was huge, far larger than a single person could hope to carry.

"Is there some event going on?" I asked with some elation, getting the impression that something special was happening.

Ginme grinned. "Today's the Kurama Fire Festival!"

"The Kurama-what-now?"

The instant I asked that, a loud voice thundered from the direction of the local head temple, Kurama-dera. "Let the ceremony begin!"

As though waiting for those words, fires began to light up all across the village.

"The fires are lit!" Kinme said happily. "Look, Suimei, look!"

"What's going on? Explain," Suimei demanded of the twins.

The ones to answer, however, were the children.

"The torches go on fire!"

"The kids go first!"

"The kids what? What do you—"

Before Suimei could finish, Sora and Umi jumped off the roof and glided down. They approached a group of children walking while holding up a giant torch and, to my surprise, joined them.

I was worried their Tengu appearance would cause alarm, but

such worries proved unnecessary as they both seemed to go un-
noticed by normal humans, blending in naturally.

"Yay!"

"It's hot!"

They smiled and waved at us.

After watching all that unfold, and seeing how we became
quite confused in the process, Ginme decided to give us a proper
explanation. "The festival starts with small torches being held
by kids, with bigger torches appearing as it continues. The final
torch needs tons of adults to carry."

"Oh... I see. Isn't it dangerous for kids to hold torches, though?"

"Their parents are with them, so it should be fine."

He pointed to a few other places in the village and began explaining some things about the Kurama Fire Festival. It occurred
annually every October 22nd and was considered one of Kyoto's
Three Great Strange Festivals. The tradition was thought to have
started in the third year of the Tengyo era (the year 940 by the
Gregorian calendar) when the Yuki Daimyojin deity, previously
enshrined in the imperial palace in ancient Kyoto, was moved to
Kurama.

"This festival's amazing. We come out every year to watch it."

"Is that so?"

"It all started with some people long ago who were impressed
by the procession for the moving of the Yuki Daimyojin, and
they've kept it up since. It's incredible." Ginme wore a faint
smile as he watched a mother help a few children carry a small
torch.

Eventually, the children all walked past, and a line of men carrying large, long objects that resembled giant bludgeons took their place. Those were torches too, apparently. Each required multiple people to support, their hot flames flaking wildly as the men continued along.

"Saireya, Sairyou!" The men chanted what equated to "festival, festival" as they vigorously and imposingly made their way through the village. They wore sendo-gote over their arms—a type of clothing typically worn by ferrymen to emphasize arm strength—as well as zori and hanten, thonged sandals and short winter coats. The tourists watched, spellbound, and directed their cameras toward them.

After some time, the rhythmic pounding of taiko drums played by women began to reverberate through the town, and the festival took on a whole new fervor. Areas were blockaded as police officers arrived to guide a group of people wearing a style of dress seldom seen.

"Whoa! Look at that!" I said.

The people wore hakama adorned with family crests, as well as full plate armor, and walked in line with the ones holding the torches. It was as though I were being given a glimpse of the past.

"It's like Kyoto's Festival of the Ages... Whoa, h-hey!"

Ginme abruptly picked me up.

"Wh-what are you doing?!"

"The main event's about to begin! We're moving to get a better view!"

"W-wait, at least let me ride piggyback—aaah!"

He ignored me and rose into the air with a gust of his wings, leaping across the rooftops. The sudden up and down motions dizzied me, until eventually I got fed up and said, "Wait, wait, wait! What about Umi and Sora?! Are we just leaving them?!"

"They'll come on their own later. Nyaa, Kinme, don't fall behind!" Carrying me under his arm, Ginme ran like the wind. Nyaa-san and Kinme fell farther and farther behind, eventually falling out of sight completely.

"Ginme, you're going too fast for everyone!" I warned.

"Don't worry, Kinme knows where we're going. They won't get lost."

"Okay, but at least put me on your back—*eeeek!*" I shrieked as he kicked hard off a rooftop. It would have been nice if he changed how he was carrying me, but a certain youthful gleam in his eyes told me there was no way he was going to notice my distress anytime soon. Even since way back, he had often been carried away and become oblivious to his surroundings in just this manner.

I abandoned all hope of being moved to a more comfortable position and instead tried to at least find out where we were headed. "Where are we going?!"

"Hm? To where all the torches are being gathered!" He made another big leap off a rooftop.

"Ugh." I kept my mouth shut so I wouldn't bite my tongue and resigned myself to just watching the surroundings pass me by. The ancient village looked beautiful, illuminated by torches; it had a certain charm that was missing from the spirit realm's perpetual night.

The light of the flickering flames was utterly different from the selfish, immediate glow of the glimmerflies. The flames were powerful and captivating. One couldn't help but stare, blinding though they were.

*It's beautiful,* I thought to myself. *Humans really know how to live it up.* Entranced by this world, so completely different from my own, I found myself forgetting that I too was a human. I watched the people celebrating their peculiar tradition with beaming smiles and thought to myself that they too were blinding.

"Saireya, Sairyou!"

As I listened to the chants of the procession, a terribly familiar figure entered my view.

*Whoa, whoa, whoa, whoa!* I shook my head in disbelief. This wasn't the spirit realm. I must have mistaken what I saw for something else...

"Saireya, Sairyou!" Chanting alongside the torch-carrying men was a monstrously huge one-eyed oni. He was at least three times taller than the humans walking alongside him. With each step he took, I worried he might crush somebody.

"Wh-wh-what, why...?" Flustered, I scanned the area, at which point I was taken aback by all I had failed to notice earlier.

"Bwa ha ha ha! Saireya, Sairyou!"

"Ha ha, look at that human! He looks so funny!"

The ancient streets of Kurama Village were brimming with excitement—so much so that nobody noticed the spirits mixed in with the spectators here and there. An Onibaba sipped sake from a wooden shoe box as she stood between two humans watching the event while hunched over their second-story window. An Okuri Suzume bird spirit rhythmically hopped atop a taiko drum. Looking up, I saw a giant shadow looking down over the town—an Onyudo. They all smiled, watching the fire festival happily together with the locals and tourists.

*Where could all these spirits have popped out from? Didn't most of them move to the spirit realm...?*

That was when it hit me: They had returned just to see this festival. I felt my face soften into a smile. As the times changed, spirits did leave; but that didn't mean they'd forgotten the human world.

*It's like a visit home for the holidays,* I thought. Something about that made me a little happy...and a little envious.

"Is this their place to return to?" I whispered my thoughts. I felt a tinge of sadness as I watched the scene fade into the distance behind me.

We eventually reached our destination, the main temple gate of Kurama-dera.

The temple gate, usually a solemn place, was brimming with excitement. A shimenawa rope cordoning off consecrated ground was stretched out. A group of men holding torches crowded together while another group of men watched as they chanted and clapped their hands in rhythm.

"Saireya, Sairyou... Saireya, Sairyou..."

The torches lit up the night, making it as bright as midday. Sparks fell like rain onto the men holding the torches, and for a moment I worried they were too hot. But even hotter yet was everyone's zeal, so much so that I couldn't help but utter, "Amazing..."

"Right?" Ginme said.

The zeal of the people, the brilliance of the flames, the billowing white smoke—the beauty of this scene, which could simply never be recreated in daytime, was like something pulled from another world.

The fervor reached its peak as all the torches were grouped into one pile. Cheers echoed as each torch added caused the licks of flames to stretch higher. Each and every person present watched the fire, enthralled.

"Looks like it's my time to shine," Ginme said.

"Huh...?"

He grinned, then moved me so I was carried in both of his arms. "Sorry, being carried like that must've been scary."

"So you *did* notice! ...Wait, more importantly, what are you trying to do now? I said wait!"

Without paying me any mind, he spread his pitch-black wings and flapped them, lifting off into the air and flying toward the giant bonfire.

"Wait—aaaaaaaaaah!"

"'Scuse me, Tengu coming through!" He stopped just before the bonfire and started flying around it in circles, close enough to touch the flames. The crackling fire began to rise abnormally high; the embers swirled as though alive.

Everyone's jaw dropped. Not a single gust of wind blew

through the area, yet the flames were being stoked. It was a mystery to behold.

Ginme got increasingly carried away and began spinning even faster. "Aha ha ha ha ha ha ha ha! How's that?!"

"Aaaaah!" I clung for dear life to Ginme, shutting my eyes and hoping he would hurry up and finish whatever he was trying to do.

Eventually, after some more flying in circles, he did finish, landing below. He let me go, and I fell to the ground, knees weak. He paid me no mind and looked up at the pillar of fire reaching up to the heavens with a satisfied look on his face.

I heard voices begin murmuring nearby. "Incredible. But why'd it grow so suddenly? Did someone toss in gasoline or something?"

"No way. Nobody'd be that stupid..."

They all tried to reason out why the flames had strengthened so suddenly, suggesting that maybe someone had put something in the torches, or a localized whirlwind had occurred, but nobody could produce a satisfying explanation. That was, until a person said, "Hey... You think this might be the work of one of Mount Kurama's Tengu?"

I looked at Ginme in shock. He smiled a toothy smile at me and made the peace sign. This had been his plan all along.

With some excitement, more and more people gradually came to agree with the idea.

"Yeah, that just might be it! This *is* the land of the Tengu, after all!"

"Oh, so it was the Tengu, huh?"

"Maybe... Yeah."

The idea gradually seeped through the crowd, until even the people that gave more scientific reasonings had come to agree. Before long, one man said, "The Tengu's telling us that he's enjoying the festival too! All right, people! Let's liven things up!"

"Yeah!"

The men began with renewed vigor, chanting, "Saireya, Sairyou," and clapping their hands loudly as though trying to show off to whatever Tengu might be watching.

Then it happened. The flames grew in intensity, *without* Ginme doing anything. The people cheered as their excitement was amped up even further. I watched everything unfold with blank astonishment.

"Heh heh. Relics of the past? Forgotten by humans?" Ginme suddenly began. "What a load of bull. There's no doubt in my mind that the Tengu exist to these people here and now."

He bumped his fist atop my head. "Sure, some of us spirits have disappeared, but just look at this festival. It all started years ago, yet people still keep it going to this day. What will remain, will remain, and what won't, won't. That's all there is to it. And it's not like what's gone is gone forever either... Who knows; those forgotten spirits might return someday."

Feeling like I might cry, I clamped my lips shut tight. Seeing this, he looked down at me gently and said, "It's all right. It's nothing you need to worry about."

"Yeah..." I quickly tried to wipe away the tears welling up in my eyes. "I want to help spirits read more. There's so many good books out there."

"I know."

"So, I'm going to keep trying. It's...okay if I keep trying, right?"

"Of course. I'll be there to help you."

I sniffed. "Thank you, Ginme."

He showed me another toothy smile and extended his hand. "The festival has only just begun. They're going to carry out the mikoshi next, let's go watch!"

"Yeah!"

"They carry these guys in fundoshi with their legs spread open like a 'V' alongside the mikoshi. It's pretty cool."

"Th-they do *what*?! No way."

"I'm serious. It's called choppen. Apparently, it's an old coming-of-age ceremony. Crazy, huh?" Saying that, Ginme carried me—piggyback this time, thank goodness—and flew off.

Sure enough, there was a crowd formed over by the stone steps. It had been a while since I'd seen a mikoshi, a portable shrine carried by a group of people, so seeing one now made me a bit excited.

That was when Nyaa-san and the others finally caught up. "Jeez! Where were you two?!" she said.

"My bad, my bad," Ginme said. "But Kinme, you should've known the route. Why didn't you lead them to us?"

"Well... I didn't want to get in the way of your moment."

I ignored the three fussing back and forth and called out to Suimei, limply sprawled out on Nyaa-san's back. "Still not good with flying, I take it?" I asked.

"Shut it. You'd have to be nuts to be okay with this. Even roller coasters come with safety bars," he complained.

"Aha ha! Let's take it easy after the festival then. It's been a busy day."

"Humph..."

Just then, I felt someone's eyes watching me. I looked to see Ginme watching Suimei and I talk. "Ginme? What's up?" I asked.

"Naw, it's nothing." He lightly shook his head. "All right! This festival's just getting started!" he crowed before rising even higher into the air.

The Kurama Fire Festival went until midnight.

We stayed until the very end, only then returning to the abandoned temple, dead tired. I dove into bed and slept like a log, ignoring the smell of smoke clinging to my body.

The next morning, I helped out with cleaning around the temple and ate a nice helping of Kyoto-style pickled foods for breakfast. I finished off by taking a dip in the hot springs at Kurama Onsen to rest my body and soul.

A festival, good food, and a hot spring. I thought I had come to air out books, but here I was acting like any old tourist. Oh well. It was a good two days.

I went to say farewell to Kinme and Ginme. "Thanks for all the help, you two. Can you give Sojobo my thanks for me?"

"Will do, Kaori!" Ginme said.

"Is it all right if I come again the next time I need to air the books out?" I asked.

"Of course," Kinme confirmed. "We'll try to keep the temple grounds clear for you for real this time."

I turned to leave when Ginme suddenly called after me. "Hey, Kaori?"

"Yes?" I asked.

He pulled me a short distance away and mumbled, "Uh, are you and uh... Are you and Suimei, uh..." He averted his eyes awkwardly.

"What's up?"

"W-well..." He hemmed and hawed. "N-nothing. Yeah, nothing. Don't worry about it," he said unconvincingly, waving his hands.

Worried, I asked, "Is something wrong?"

"Well, not quite wrong, but..." He hesitated again.

I stood on my toes and stretched to rub the top of his head. Humored by how much he'd outgrown me, I smiled. "It's all right, Ginme. You can tell me anything. We're practically family."

"Right, family..." he said before letting out a deep sigh. It wasn't like him to sigh, what with how upbeat he was all the time. But just when I thought something might be wrong, he immediately cheered up and declared, "Oh, fine! I've just got to get out of the family-zone first!"

"The family-zone? What's that?" I asked.

"Don't worry about it!" He roared with laughter, slapping me hard on the back.

Krik—a sharp, loud sound echoed throughout the mountain.

With tears in my eyes, I glared up at Ginme. "What was that for?!"

# Playing with Butterflies and Becoming Human

**T**HERE WERE TIMES I had to ask myself: Was I really human? Ever since childhood, I was constantly told to suppress my emotions. Being bound to an Inugami meant feeling jealousy toward another would cause them pain, ruin, and sickness. As jealousy stemmed from emotions, I had to not feel anything in order to live a normal life.

But I'd never actually seen someone else suffer because of me.

The reason was simple. A slight curl of my lips, a small frown, a light crease in my brow—the slightest hint of any emotion whatsoever led the adults I knew to gather around and scold me. Nobody ever gave me the leeway to show emotion, so I never knew if showing any feeling would truly hurt someone. I wondered countless times: What if this whole thing was just a dated myth, or maybe even a lie?

They treated my emotions as though they were sins, surrounding me, scolding me. I remember I would cover my face with my small hands and beg for their forgiveness.

*"I won't smile. I won't cry. I won't be angry. So please, stop yelling..."*

*"You must not feel!" "You must not feel!" "You must not feel!"*

*"I haven't felt jealous toward anyone, so please, let me feel something, just a little bit..."*

*"For your own sake—you must suppress your self!"*

For my own sake...

Was it for *my* sake...?

That doubt clung to the back of my mind.

Life was difficult then. I had to suppress my emotions, my mind, my own being. But that was all in the past now; I didn't need to suppress my emotions anymore. Even so, I still found it difficult to express myself, perhaps due to my upbringing. I feared I might hurt somebody.

*"It'd be a bit of a problem if you hurt a client, so just suck it up and endure it."*

I remembered my father's voice clearly. He always held me in his burly arms and whispered into my ear with a twisted smile. I could still feel it all now: his lukewarm breath against my earlobe, the smell of alcohol that made me want to pinch my nose, his uncomfortable body heat against my back, even his bony hands that he would run through my hair, which had lost its color.

I would resist the urge to cover my ears as best as I could as I waited out what felt like eternity.

*Hey, Suimei. You're the last of us bound to the Inugami. Your deadweight mother's gone and kicked it, leaving just you behind to take care of the household. Got it?*

Just feel nothing. Throw away your emotions. Become an exorcist and go earn money to make your father happy.

I remember how his words echoed around my lightless cell like a whispered curse: *Just become a puppet, Suimei. A puppet that'll move however I like...*

Oh... Come to think of it, whenever I talked to someone back then, they always wore a specific pair of emotions on their face—fear and disgust. Perhaps it was only natural. My hair was white, and I made no expressions. That, coupled with the fact that I could order around an Inugami, a being beyond human understanding, made fear and disgust perfectly understandable.

I asked myself again: Was I really human? What sin must I have committed to be forbidden from what is permitted to all?

Perhaps I was wrong to assume I was ever human at all.

*Yes... Yes, that must be it. I'm sure even now countless white strings are stretching down from the clouds above to bind my entire being.*

"My, that's some nasty swelling; I'll get you some medicine, dear. Suimei, could you fix some up for me please?"

"Sure."

"Kuro, could you be a darling and bring sweets out for our guest?"

"Yes!"

I prepared the necessary medicine as Noname cheerfully chatted up the patient, Akaname—a spirit that liked to lick the filth in bathtubs and bathrooms.

Akaname, who had come because of a terrible mouth ulcer, let out a sigh of relief and lowered her head. "Oh, I'm so relieved you can help. Thank you... Licking filth's been so hard because of this ulcer."

"You've been overworking yourself," Noname chided. "Rest a bit, give your body the break it deserves."

"I want to, I really do. But I just can't bring myself to stop... You wouldn't believe how much grime builds up in the baths of men who live alone." Akaname flopped around her long and slimy tongue, then winced, likely because of the ulcer.

Noname ran a hand through Akaname's moss-green hair, crossed the long legs jutting out of her Chinese-style dress, and smiled. "Just trust me and rest for a few days. You'll be thankful you did," she said with a coquettish wink.

That gesture, combined with her feminine charms, was enough to fluster most people. She had clear amber eyes, long moss-green hair, a head notably smaller than a normal person's, and a pair of twisting bull horns on her head—an appearance certainly unique by human standards, though I doubt any human would deny her attractiveness. If a gullible man had been on the receiving end of that wink just now, he'd be head over heels for sure.

Unfortunately, the recipient was Akaname, a spirit with the form of a withered old lady. Far from charmed, she chuckled at the wink and shrugged. "Well, all right. I guess I could rest for a short while."

"I'll give you some ointment for your ulcer, as well as some medicine to drink. If it doesn't heal by the time you run out, please do come again. It'll be a problem if it's actually a more serious ailment."

Akaname smiled broadly and nodded.

Strictly speaking, the spirit realm had no doctors. This was because most spirits chose to heal their own injuries, even the serious ones. This was especially true for spirits living in nature, like the Kijimuna. Spirits were more akin to wild animals than people in that regard.

But in town, we had an apothecary. Many spirits who lived here crossed to and from the human world and were used to receiving medical treatment, which had created a demand for the apothecary's services. The apothecary sold medicine like any normal apothecary, but this one was unique in that it also offered simple medical treatment. It was run by a nameless spirit who we simply called Noname, an enigmatic woman who seemed vaguely Chinese. She had invited me to work with her after I reunited with Kuro and quit my job as an exorcist.

"Whew! That's the last check-up for the day. Good work, both of you." With Akaname having left, Noname stretched her back.

With autumn's arrival, business had picked up from all the spirits coming to stock up on medicine for the winter. The worst of it had already passed though, and the last few days had been fairly slow.

"Come join me for tea in the courtyard, Suimei. Kuro-chan should already be setting up. You don't mind waiting until after tea to make dinner, do you?"

"Not at all." I left the medicine mixing table behind and headed for the courtyard.

The inside of the apothecary had a foreign feel. There were Chinese-style transom windows with patterns complex yet beautiful, vivid red trinkets decorating various shelves, and a number of small, square medicine cabinets positioned around the medicine mixing table.

The cabinets lined the white, clay wall behind it and contained a myriad of glass containers holding ingredients for making medicine. A mortar and pestle sat atop the medicine mixing table, as well as a list of medicines and their effects. This spot alone smelled different from the rest of the shop.

Farther back, there was a courtyard surrounded by buildings on all sides. I recalled this being common in China, particularly in Beijing. *Siheyuan*, I believe it was called—a type of family home layout where rooms were situated in the four cardinal directions around a courtyard.

Noname, the owner of the house, lived in the north main room. Kuro and I were borrowing the east room. The west room was where Noname kept her massive collection of clothes, and the south room was the apothecary.

"Suimei! Over here, over here!" Kuro called for me the moment I stepped out into the courtyard. On the table was the Chinese tea Noname was so proud of.

I leisurely made my way toward Kuro. A sweet scent tickled my nose, coming from the tea olives planted in the courtyard. The season for flowers should be ending soon, but the white petals peering out from between the deep-green leaves still wafted strongly. Tea olives had a gentler scent than fragrant olives. Sweet, but not overbearingly so.

The tea olives weren't the only thing adorning the courtyard, however. Autumnal flowers that could be used for medicine were planted everywhere, filling the courtyard with color. There were autumn bellflowers, great burnets, red spider lilies... Strange as it was, they all seemed to outlive their human world counterparts.

Starlight shone down on the fragrant courtyard, and a birdcage holding glimmerflies hung suspended from the passage leading up to it. This courtyard—lit only by the faint shimmers of stars and glimmerflies, and brimming with the scent of autumn—was a place where I always felt welcome.

"My, I'm thirsty." Not long after I had taken a seat, Noname appeared. She hummed a tune as she poured out a cup of tea and drank it in one gulp. "Whew! That hits the spot. Nothing beats tea after a day of work!"

In a blink, her bewitching charm vanished. This prompted Kuro to whisper, "She's kinda like an old man downing a drink after work, huh?"

Noname looked over at Kuro and gave him a charming smile. She then picked him up with a well-muscled arm and opened her third eye. "Fine! Biologically, I'm a man! But my heart is that of a maiden, so think twice before making such senseless comments! A maiden's heart is as fragile as tofu!"

"Lies! Your heart is made out of concrete!" Kuro exclaimed.

"Even concrete can be easily broken by an excavator!"

"But it's not fragile if you need an excavator?!"

Right. So...Noname was an older guy with the appearance of a young woman. Dressing like a woman seemed to be her hobby. In her own words, "Being a woman is more convenient." As for what it was more convenient for...I figured I was better off not knowing.

Kuro's and Noname's yelling echoed through the courtyard. Kuro was fairly reserved when we'd first started living here, but he had become more outspoken as of late. He'd had a tummy ache recently, but other than that, he seemed to be enjoying life more. Although, I doubted he'd have much longer to enjoy it if he kept making thoughtless comments about Noname...

"You may be a middle-aged guy, but you're prettier than any-one I know! It's so confusing! Like, what is gender anyway?! Jeez!" Kuro groaned.

"Hm...? Oh. You think I'm pretty?" Noname said.

"Duh?! Who wouldn't?" Kuro said, his tail whisking in the air.

Noname made a not wholly dissatisfied smile and lowered Kuro onto a chair. She then put some teacake in front of him. "For you, Kuro-chan."

"Yay! I can have this?! Yahoo!"

*Well, all's well that ends well.* This wasn't the first time that one of Kuro's thoughtless comments had gotten him in trouble with Noname, and it wasn't the first time his natural airheaded-ness had saved him either. I just let things play out at this point.

"Oh, that reminds me, Suimei..." Noname suddenly began. She looked me over while holding a teacup in hand. "Have you been sleeping okay as of late?"

Truthfully, I hadn't. Being startled awake by dreams of the past had become a normal occurrence for me recently. But how did Noname know that from all the way in her room? "...What makes you think that?"

"I can hear you moaning and groaning from across the compound. Would you like me to make you some medicine?"

"Huh?"

"Medicine. For your sleep. I can prepare you some with more mild effects. You could even start drinking it today."

My lack of sleep certainly did leave me exhausted. But I was fine with that. I preferred not to risk falling into a deep sleep while in the spirit realm. This was a world rampant with spirits who ate humans, and I had no intent to let my guard down.

I answered, "No, I'm okay."

"Are you sure?"

"Yeah."

"Well, all right..." She smiled sadly.

That was when somebody entered the courtyard through the apothecary. "Oh, there you two are! Evening!"

She had a bob cut dyed brown, perfectly round chestnut-colored eyes, a roundish nose, and wore a plaid dress with the warm colors of autumn. She was Muramoto Kaori, the girl who lived at the bookstore, and a human like me.

Kaori met my eyes and smiled, waving gleefully at me.

*Ugh.*

Kuro hopped onto my knees. "Kaori-chan! What're you here for?" he asked.

"Kuro! Aw, you're so cute. I'm here to get some medicine from Noname."

"Oooh. Well, you're free to join us. The tea tastes great!"

"Will do!" Kaori happily took the seat next to me and began talking about whatever with Noname.

I quietly let out a sigh of relief and looked away from her. That was when Kuro whispered, "Are you all right? Are you nervous because Kaori's here?"

"...As if."

"Oh?" Still on my lap, Kuro tilted his head to the side and looked up at me with his cute puppy dog eyes.

I...didn't dislike Kaori. If anything, I felt indebted to her and wanted to repay her one day. But I just couldn't help but flounder before her smile. It made my chest feel tight—not in a painful way, but tight nonetheless. Maybe I felt jealous of how she could so easily express the emotions I couldn't.

"Don't worry, Suimei! I'll do all the talking; you can just nod your head and listen!"

*Who does this dog think he is?* I sighed, reached for his neck, and gently stroked it. "Don't be an idiot."

"Oooh?! Oooh..." Kuro collapsed flat on my knees, squirming with joy as I scratched the perfect spot.

*You're a hundred years too early to be teasing me, Kuro,* I thought to myself when, suddenly, I felt someone's gaze and looked up.

"You two always get along well. You're practically joined at the hip." It was Kaori, smiling broadly at us.

Feeling bashful, I frowned. "...This is normal. We're partners."

"Right, right."

Something about the way she watched us so joyously, it irritated me.

It appeared she could tell, as she giggled and said, "Sorry, am I interrupting your moment with Kuro?"

"Let's put that aside," I said, trying to change the topic. "You said you came for medicine? Are you feeling sick?"

She shook her head. "I'm here to pick up some butterfly repellent. I'll be making a delivery tomorrow and need to drink it or I'll be swarmed by the swarms of glimmerflies over there."

"Oh, I see. That makes sense." I looked over at the birdcage hanging in the passageway. A number of ghostly butterflies known as glimmerflies were caged within it. Glimmerflies were used in place of lights in this world of perpetual night. They emitted no heat yet glowed brighter than fire. They burned out and faded over time, however, so butterfly hunters had to constantly hunt more to replenish them.

Glimmerflies did more than just glow, though. They were also drawn to humans. Kaori and I were human, and as such, we were swarmed by glimmerflies whenever we went outside. The apothecary lit special butterfly repellent incense made by Noname, but if we went someplace without the incense, the glimmerflies gathered around and illuminated the place so brightly that you might think you were in the human world.

Whether one liked it or not, the glimmerflies made humans stand out like a sore thumb. Perhaps that was why so few humans lived in the spirit realm. You had to be born under a lucky star to manage to survive all the human-eating spirits, what with the glimmerflies constantly pointing you out like a spotlight. Conversely, you could say it would have been easy to live here if it weren't for the glimmerflies.

"I wonder why glimmerflies are drawn to humans anyway..." I mused.

"Who knows. Kinda weird, huh? Maybe we smell different?" Kaori sniffed her arm.

Perhaps the glimmerflies *were* attracted to a human-specific pheromone. *This might be worth looking into.*

That was when Noname suddenly said, "Oh, Suimei! You should go with Kaori!"

I glared daggers her way. Every now and then, Noname made these outrageous, whimsical suggestions. Just the other day, in fact, she had suggested I go to Okinawa—well, *forced* me to go, I should say.

"Can't," I said. "Tomorrow's a workday."

"Oh, don't worry about the shop. We've hardly had any customers as of late; I can manage on my lonesome. You should go. There's *much* for you to learn there." There was an indecipherable glimmer behind her clear amber gaze.

I frowned, unnerved by Noname's behavior. This didn't seem to be one of her whimsical suggestions after all. My intuition as a former exorcist told me something was up. "...What do you mean by 'much to learn'?" I asked.

"I meant just that. Nothing more."

Noname was shrouded in mystery. She might have raised Kaori like a mother, but a spirit was a spirit. I couldn't trust her as easily as Kaori could, no matter how much goodwill she had shown me.

"You really should go, Suimei," she said. I couldn't help but feel there was something fishy about her smile.

*Just what could she be planning?*

Just as my mind began to race, a blithe voice rang out. "Wait, Suimei's coming? That's great!"

It was Kaori. I clicked my tongue, peeved by her attitude. How could she be so carefree when there was clearly something lying in wait for us? *...I have to protect her.*

I sighed and confirmed that I would be joining Kaori. Noname smiled and nodded. A little sadly, she said, "...That's good. You two enjoy yourselves now."

The next morning, Kuro and I met up with Kaori and the black cat at the edge of town. The black cat had already transformed to the size of a tiger and was carrying a cloth bundle of books—what I assumed to be our delivery—on her back.

"Morning, Suimei. Did you drink the butterfly-repellent tonic?" Kaori asked.

"Yeah. Are we going through a hell again?"

"Nope. Our destination's not that far this time."

"I see." I gave her a slight nod and felt for the pouch at my waist.

It contained purifying salt, sacred sake, and talismans. If it came down to it, I was prepared to use these to fight alongside Kuro. That being said, I hadn't prepared these things specifically for today. I actually kept this pouch on me whenever I went outside. It would have been crazy to walk around unarmed with all these spirits.

"I may not be an exorcist anymore...but I haven't lost my edge," I muttered.

"Hm? Did you say something, Suimei?"

"No, nothing." I shook my head. Kaori trusted spirits. She'd have been disappointed to know I had these things on me, and I had no particular need to tell her. She'd grown up in the spirit realm, while I'd made a living by hunting spirits in the human world. As sad as it was to say, we saw spirits differently.

The black cat slowly waltzed over to Kuro, shot him a dangerous look, and said, "I'll allow you to come along, mutt, but...you better not get in the way of our work."

"Are you looking down on me?! Do you think you're hot stuff now just 'cause you're a little bigger, huh?!" Kuro didn't cower in the face of the much larger black cat.

She stared at him with her mismatched sky-blue and gold eyes before letting out an exasperated sigh. "...You sure talk big for someone with their tail between their legs."

Kuro let out a sharp whine and hid behind me, embarrassed to be outed. He peered back at the black cat from between my legs.

Those two really had the worst chemistry... No, maybe that wasn't quite it.

"Heh heh. That's right, mutt."

Maybe it would have been more apt to say that Kuro had become the black cat's toy?

I warned the black cat not to tease Kuro too much and asked that we be on our way.

Our destination really wasn't that far from town at all. In just thirty minutes, we had come to a dense forest, and in no time, Kaori led us to a large lake within it.

"Look at that! It's beautiful, right, Suimei?" she boastfully declared upon arrival.

No winds were present that day, letting the surface of the lake stand still from end to end. Like a polished mirror, it reflected the reddish autumn sky of the spirit realm, ever so slightly changing color as the sky did. In the center of the lake was a small island, and on that island was some sort of building. For some strange reason, the island appeared brighter than its surroundings. Leading to it was a red bridge, connecting shore to shore.

The lake stretched as far as I could see, almost like an ocean. Maybe it was the darkness, but the water seemed to seamlessly bleed into the sky on the horizon. The sky and the lake unified into a pool of innumerable stars. It was as if the starry sky enclosed us from all directions.

Kaori was right; it was beautiful. But that was no reason to let my guard down.

It looked safe at first glance, but I could only think that we would be sitting ducks if assaulted from the lake or the air while traversing the bridge. "Be careful," I warned her.

"I'm not gonna fall off the bridge! Don't treat me like a child!" she complained in return.

*That's not what I mean.* That was what I wanted to say, but I realized it wouldn't be worth the effort to explain and instead sighed. Kaori began walking across the bridge without a care in the world, and I followed closely behind, monitoring our surroundings carefully.

The bridge looked ancient, but it was sturdy. Our footsteps reverberated on it as if it were a springy taiko drum.

Out of breath, Kaori yelled at the black cat, now walking quite a ways ahead of us. "Slow down, Nyaa-san! We can't keep up!"

"No way. Do you know how heavy these things are?" The black cat sounded eager to unload the package on her back and continued farther along.

"Jeez... She always just does what she likes." Kaori quickly gave up, accustomed to the black cat's behavior. She sighed deeply, then continued crossing at her own leisurely pace.

That was when Kuro, walking in front, let out a surprised murmur. "Whoa... What is this?" he said as he looked down into the lake from over the bridge.

Curious, I looked down as well. The lake should have been considerably deep, yet somehow, the water was clear enough to see all the way into its depths. Aquatic creatures swayed in the water and brilliant red fish with long tails, perhaps goldfish, swam in schools between them.

"No..." I muttered in disbelief.

Beyond the schools of fish was an impossible sight: An enormous single-story building. It was a bit peculiar in that it lacked a roof, exposing everything inside, and it looked like a decoration one would find in an aquarium.

But this was clearly no decoration, for a number of living spaces filled the enormous building. They were of simple design, tatami-matted and housing only bedding, but they were each filled by white-robed humans. The majority laid down asleep, unmoving. They looked sickly pale, many of them thin. The ones who were awake curled up and hugged their knees, blankly staring off at nothing in particular.

On one side of each room was something I had seldom seen before—a wooden lattice grid, reminiscent of zashiki cells, an Edo-era prison used to confine criminals and the mad.

I felt goosebumps cover my body and went stiff with fear, like I had just seen something I wasn't meant to have seen. I rubbed my eyes to make sure there wasn't anything wrong with them.

*There's no way humans would be here. Am I dreaming?*

A glimmerfly fluttered into view, reminding me that this was no dream. Pulled back into reality, I became acutely aware of the disgust rising within me.

*What did I just see? What are humans doing here of all places?*

Everything clicked into place at once. It was so obvious. This world only appeared like mine on the bare surface. In reality, it was a plane ruled by terrible, monstrous beings known as spirits—and who knew how many spirits loved nothing more than to eat humans?

"Kaori."

"Hm? What's up?"

"What...what is this?"

"Huh?"

Sweat glided down my back. Kaori seemed unaware of the reality beneath her feet.

"Can you look at this and still call it beautiful?" Trembling, I pointed down at what lay beneath the lake.

She *laughed*. "Uh, yeah? What's not beautiful about an underwater building? Pretty much the only place you'd find one too."

I recoiled a few steps. Kuro swiftly ran up to me and, with his head lowered, growled at Kaori.

*What is going on? What is wrong with her?!* Fearful, I reached for my pouch.

Kaori was alien to me. Having been raised in the spirit realm, her sensibilities confounded me often. That wasn't particularly unusual. Culture shock was common, even between those of the same country. This world belonged to the spirits, so there was likely much I didn't understand.

But humans being raised like cattle? That was something I could *never* accept!

"Suimei? Kuro?"

*Just what the hell* is *Kaori? I thought she was a human like me, but she's not. She's, she's—*a monster.

The moment that word crossed my mind, I swallowed hard. I was appalled that I could think such a thing about her.

About Kaori.

"Hey, what's wrong?" Confused, she reached out for me. I reflexively backed away, causing her to flinch.

"Ah..." My chest felt tight. *I* had been the one to hurt *her*, so why did my heart ache so much?

I then realized my grave error. I had rejected her merely because I couldn't understand her. How was I any better than all those people who had looked at me with fear and disgust in their eyes?

"My, my," a voice said with some exasperation. From behind Kaori, I saw a person walk along the bridge toward us, coming from the direction of the small island.

I immediately pulled talismans out of my pouch and hid them out of view, clutched in my palm. Kaori turned around and...greeted the person by name.

"Yao Bikuni..."

"Hello, Kaori. I see quite the something's going on between you two..."

The person, a woman, had a Buddhist nun hood on and wore a black and purple rakusu—a monastic waistcoat—that hung from her neck. She held an elaborate smoking pipe in her right hand and a long line of prayer beads coiled around her wrist. She looked to be a nun, as the name Yao Bikuni—literally "the eight-hundred-year-old nun"—suggested, but she seemed far too young and beautiful to live up to the number.

"I take it that it's your first time coming here, young man?" she said. "Then it's no wonder you're so alarmed. Only those experiencing this place for the first time perceive its uncanny nature.

Ah, a terrifying thing it is, to unknowingly grow so accustomed to something that you become blind to its strangeness. But at the same time, is it not a blessing as gentle as a mother's love? If experiencing new things invokes such discomfort, perhaps it'd be best to never have to experience anything new at all, no?"

The Buddhist nun snickered softly. She looked to be at the peak of her youth but spoke with the profundity of someone much older. She had a subdued air that didn't match her apparent age and gave off a sense of cunning that one could only hope to obtain through experience.

She put her smoking pipe to her lips, puffed, and blew out white smoke. "Young man, I have no responsibility to correct your wild misunderstandings. But I will this time, out of consideration for Kaori. This place is not what you imagine it to be. This place is where scarred souls come to rest. No living humans reside here...much less any meant for consumption."

Saying no more, she turned toward the small island. She looked back over her shoulder; her grin warped her beautiful face. "But that isn't to say you should let your guard down while you're here. Enjoy your stay, young man."

We were greeted by yet more fresh sights after crossing the bridge. Just past a torii gate that must have been constructed from a massive tree, there stood countless wooden grave tablets unceremoniously stuck into the ground all over the all-too-small island, like candles on a birthday cake.

In the center of the island was a temple onto which annexes

had been haphazardly added. It was an ugly thing, towering three stories high. The main doors were closed, concealing whatever Buddha idols might be enshrined inside. I had to ask: Would a twisted place like this even contain anything to worship? If it did, the deities had to be equally warped.

Regardless, the most striking thing about the island was the number of butterflies. The roof of the temple, the great willows beside it, the ground, the grave tablets—glimmerflies rested atop each and every place imaginable. I finally understood why the butterfly-repellent tonic was so necessary. Any human who wandered in here would be swarmed, and quite possibly die of asphyxiation.

The caretaker of this utterly abnormal land was a *former* human, Yao Bikuni. Yao Bikuni had once been a normal village girl until one day, as a child, she ate the mermaid flesh her father had brought home, thus ceasing to be human and becoming immortal. She looked young, but her true age was over eight hundred. Walking alongside such a nun, rich with history, we stepped foot on land.

The moment we left the bridge, I apologized. "Kaori, I'm sorry."

"No, it's my fault for not explaining more. I was so used to this place that I didn't stop and think how it might seem to someone else." She looked relieved and put a hand to her chest. "Still, I'm surprised. I didn't expect you to look at me like I was a total stranger."

"I'm really, really sorry."

"No, no, no, I'm not blaming you or anything," she said, waving her hands. "Everybody makes mistakes, don't worry about it! Now where did Nyaa-san go...?" She scanned the area.

I fought down the apology rushing to my lips and studied Kaori's figure from behind. I felt pathetic. The moment I'd thought she held values that differed from my own, I had rejected her. It took everything I had to not try to make excuses for myself.

I had done unto Kaori the very thing I hated the most.

She was putting on a brave front now, but I knew I had hurt her. I bit my lip and swore I would never make such a mistake again.

"Hey, can you tell me more about this place?" I asked. I needed to understand her better. That way I would never again subject her to my own baseless fears.

Kaori looked stunned for a moment, but then she broke out into a pure, genuine smile.

My chest tightened painfully, as though someone had gripped my heart. My pulse began to race. Just what was this feeling? How could Kaori's smile have such an effect on me?

She tilted her head to the side and, in a slightly playful tone, said, "All right, why don't I give Mr. New to the Spirit Realm here a crash course? Souls exist in a cycle. After death, a new life awaits each one."

Kaori went on to explain to me what Yao Bikuni had once explained to her. She talked about the endless cycle of rebirth, samsara, a belief that souls are reborn after death. There were similar beliefs across many religions, but the one Kaori spoke of was the one taught in Buddhism.

"Humans go to one of six realms after death: The heavenly realm, the human realm, the asura realm, the animal realm, the realm of hungry ghosts, and the realm we call hell. You're not always reborn as a human, but you will be reborn as something living. Here, we have souls that *should* be ready for reincarnation—however, they lack the strength they need to endure it."

"What do you mean by that?" I asked.

Yao Bikuni cut in, continuing where Kaori left off. "Their hearts became too worn in life. Goodness, just what has come of the human world? With each passing day, more and more souls refuse to be reborn, instead wishing to fade away to nothingness. Forcing such souls to experience rebirth would lead to a twisted new life, so instead we let them rest here. I suppose it's not too dissimilar from a hospital in the human world."

Yao Bikuni shrugged, then brought her smoking pipe to her lips and smiled. "It is my job to help them recover. Say, did you know there's nothing that can bind a soul? If those souls so wanted to leave, they could slip right through anything. That zashiki prison is just for show. They can depart whenever they feel like it; there's not even a ceiling."

I thought back to the listless, motionless humans I'd seen, free to leave at any moment. The only prison holding them was, in truth, their own hearts.

"We've come here to help those souls," said a familiar voice.

The black cat had appeared out of nowhere. She must have been nodding off on the roof of the temple, as she yawned hugely before approaching Kaori and dipping low—essentially demanding to have the package on her back unloaded.

Kaori grinned wryly at the black cat's attitude and began untying the cloth bundle. From inside appeared magazines, manga, comic books, novels...and even picture books.

"You're giving them books...?" I murmured. That was indeed how it seemed, but the selection ranged from utterly ancient to very recent material. Many of the older books were brown with age. I saw some novels dating from before the pre-war era, and even some incredibly ancient writings from the Edo period—perhaps older. Even for a bookworm, simply understanding some of these texts would be a struggle.

Taking a book in hand and cocking her head, Yao Bikuni grinned. "Old things do wonders for the heart, whether they be games, movies, music, or whatever. Such things are a necessity for souls, especially damaged ones. Without these, they'd just fade away."

"Wow! Miss Yao, uh... Miss Yao *Bikini*, you're saving souls? That's amazing!"

"Yao *Bikuni*, Kuro," I quietly corrected.

Yao Bikuni snickered softly, then gave us a somehow unnerving smile. "There's nothing amazing about it at all, dear. For every soul I save, there are many more I cannot."

"Oh, I see. That must be tough, seeing how saving souls is your job and all," Kuro said.

"I think nothing of it at all. It is impossible to save them all in the first place. Besides, I am not so kind." She squinted thoughtfully and looked far off into the distance. "No matter how much I try, there's no helping those that couldn't find meaning in their lives. Empty souls that arrive here are fated to fade."

I found myself a bit speechless at that.

To put it plainly, Yao Bikuni was dangling a spider's thread in hopes some would grasp it. Only those who could connect with something from their life would reach for this thread. Point being, salvation was something a person had to strive for themselves.

Although, in Akutagawa Ryunosuke's short story, *The Spider's Thread*, the one who dangled that thread was the Buddha Shakyamuni himself...

"This world is full of suffering. That's why people hug their knees and cower. People wish for nothing more than to hide in their shells and live the same lives day in, day out, never having to experience anything new. That is the easiest way to live." Yao Bikuni spoke as though salvation was impossible for such souls and exhaled another puff of white smoke. Then, as though declaring the topic over, she began to order about Kaori. "Would you bring these books inside the temple? Make that big cat lug them over. I'll pay after inspecting the goods, all right?"

"Yes, ma'am!" Kaori replied with vigor.

Yao Bikuni then looked Kaori up and down with a scrutinizing air. "And...Kaori. About those clothes..."

"Yes?"

"How can you stand to bare your legs like that? Goodness... Don't blame me if you come to regret your decisions when you wish to have children in the future. What happened to you? You hardly even used to wear skirts... Have you finally become aware of the opposite gender?"

"W-wait. Yao Bikuni, wait!" Kaori blushed and held down the hem of her dress.

But wait Yao Bikuni did not. She frowned and took another puff of her pipe, blowing white smoke out her nose, before plowing onward without a break. "Rather than dressing up for the man you like, you should be taking care of yourself so you can safely bear his children. The cold is a woman's greatest enemy, dear. Just think of the damage it'll do to your blood circulation—and how that'll hurt your future children. Oh, I know, let me give you one of my long underpants so your legs don't get cold."

"N-no, anything but that! I'll just carry over the books now!" Kaori yelled for the black cat and then fled in search of her.

"My, she ran away. Goodness me. Youths these days never listen to what their elders have to say," Yao Bikuni grumbled. It appeared she was the meddlesome sort, the kind that meant well but whom the "youths" just couldn't stand.

Without warning, she turned to me. I put myself on guard, wary of what she might say. She stared at me for a short while, before finally saying, "...Right. I'd forgotten. There's something I'd like to ask you."

"Yes?"

"You're the one that was bound to an Inugami... The exorcist, no?"

I immediately distanced myself from her. Without delay, Kuro braced himself for a fight as well, and I pulled out my talismans.

"I was," I said. "But now I work at an apothecary. I don't recall doing anything to earn the ire of a nun's spirit... What business do you have with me?"

"Oh, so you're at Noname's place, then. Well, that's far better than being an exorcist, isn't it?" Yao Bikuni looked at me as if I were a rare animal and lazily scratched the edge of her hood. "I've heard lots about you. You've lived a rough life, haven't you?"

"You know Noname? What's she told you?"

"We're only familiar because of my work. But Noname wasn't the one to tell me about you. Do you really think your employer the type to blab about an employee?"

I thought about it. As an apothecary, Noname was in a position that allowed her to learn not just my information but that of many people. But it was for that very reason that she was so tight-lipped. The same could be said for Kaori and the rest... So who had told this shrewd nun about me?

Yao Bikuni continued to stare at me, wearing an indecipherable smile. I felt sweat build in my palm and blot my talismans as my tension rose.

Then, without warning, Yao Bikuni turned away and waved a hand in the air. "Oh, never mind. And you shouldn't threaten a weak old nun with those things, you know."

Saying nothing further, she left.

*What was that just now?*

I finally untensed my body and stowed away my talismans. Kuro appeared equally as confused as me and watched Yao Bikuni walk away. That was when he noticed something else and, with a tilt of his head, said, "Huh? Hey, Suimei, isn't that Shinonome over there?"

"What?" Surprised, I followed Kuro's gaze. Sure enough, the owner of the bookstore was there. Initially, I thought he might have come for Kaori, but he was headed in the exact opposite direction from her.

I called out to him and began walking forward, but though I only looked away for a brief second, I soon completely lost sight of him. I scanned the area in search of Shinonome, at which point I noticed a gaudily dressed man standing close by.

"Oho... You're that Inugami," he said to Kuro. "What a coincidence it is to come across you here... No, coincidence isn't quite the right word; I should call this *destiny*. Yes, the more dramatic the word, the better it enriches the story." The strange man pressed his round sunglasses up with a finger and grinned at Kuro and me. Then he approached us without hesitation, his gaudy haori fluttering as he walked.

I braced myself, on guard against the strange man.

That was when Kuro suddenly yelled, "Get back, Suimei!" He moved between me and the man, baring his fangs and growling.

Sensing something wrong, I renewed my focus. "Kuro? Who is that man?"

The man's fierce eyes narrowed with glee. "Oh, I'm hurt. And here I thought you'd be in tears, thanking me. But I suppose reality isn't as simple as stories." He stifled some laughter, his eyes still homed in on us behind his round lenses.

Kuro glanced back at me and tensely said, "Do you remember what I had to do to unbind myself from the Shirai household?"

"Of course," I answered.

Kuro was an Inugami that possessed the Shirai bloodline— my bloodline. For the longest of times, he had wanted to free me from the burden placed on me by the rest of my family, but he hadn't known how. That was, until a certain person appeared before him one day.

*If you wish to free that poor boy of his bindings, you must eat the bones of one of his bloodline,* he had said.

And so, on the day I became seventeen, Kuro dug up my mother's grave and ate her bones—ending the cursed connection between Kuro and the Shirai household...and setting me free.

"You don't mean..." I swallowed.

Kuro nodded and glared back at the man. "That's the man who told me what to do."

"Oh, don't be such a stranger, addressing me as 'man' like that. I've told you my name, haven't I? Call me Tamaki." The man— Tamaki grinned vulgarly. "How do you like your freedom, young man? Do you feel better not having to suppress your emotions any- more? Are you not ecstatic to be rid of the ancient ways? Outdated beliefs are nothing but fetters that bind us down, you see. I'm sure the story you're now spinning is much more interesting than the old one." With some excitement, Tamaki spread his hands up in the air, and his eyes crinkled with spellbound delight.

A conflicted feeling stirred in me. The fact that I was able to live at all freely was thanks to this man. In a sense, I owed him a debt. But something about that was hard to accept. There was something out of place, something that told me it couldn't be that simple. Just listening to his words made my head throb like an alarm was going off inside my head. My instincts were telling me: Stay away from this man. *Do not trust this man.*

"I suppose...I should thank you, then. Thank you," I ventured.

"Ha ha. Not at all. In fact...I should be the one thanking you." Tamaki stroked his chin in good humor. Suddenly, he turned dead serious and offered me a handshake. "Thanks to you, yet another of the ancient ways have faded. I couldn't be happier. What better entertainment is there than this? I feel as though I've just read the conclusion to a masterpiece of a book!"

"I...I see." I caught a glimpse of some *need* that I couldn't comprehend through his round sunglasses and shuddered. I had only just sworn to never again let myself be swayed by a lack of understanding for their thoughts and feelings, but in this moment, I only knew that I never wanted anything to do with this man.

As I hesitated over whether to shake his hand, Kuro sharply growled. "So you were a spirit then. It's been more than ten years since we met, yet you haven't changed one bit. Did you tell me those things to destroy the Shirai household?! Was it all to remove more exorcists from this world?!"

Kuro glared at Tamaki with deep hatred in his eyes. Tamaki looked back at him curiously, lowered his outstretched hand, and shrugged. He looked down slightly and, in a rumble deeper than his already deep voice, said, "Now that's a baseless accusation. Certainly, it is up for debate whether I am *still* a human...but

I have no interest at all in exorcists and their ilk. I simply love to destroy what is old. Nothing more, nothing less. It's best you not read too deeply into things, or else the joy of stories might escape you."

Tamaki then knit his brows and looked toward me. "Young man, may I ask you one thing? Why, when you've finally been freed from your ancient bindings, are you still with this Inugami? Unless—is it haunting you? Should I teach you a way to erase it?"

"Huh...?" I asked, flummoxed.

"Oh, it's no skin off my back. I know plenty of methods for erasing man-made spirits like this one. Please, allow me. Let me help you fully break free from your past. That way, you can make an even more wonderful story." Tamaki gave me a smile as pure as snow and put a hand over his chest. "Rid yourself of that dog. That's what's—"

"No!" I interrupted, shielding Kuro behind my body and glaring at Tamaki. "I chose to stay with Kuro myself. He's my friend."

Tamaki raised a surprised eyebrow and sized me up. "Oho... Is that all?"

"Wh-what? Are you not finished? Leave us alone," I demanded.

"Hmm... Heh. Ha ha ha! Oh, of course! Of course, of course!" Tamaki howled with laughter. His clouded right eye looked over at me—and in an instant, he went stony, like his excitement had spontaneously dried up. "Allow me to retract my earlier statement. From the rings under your eyes and the lukewarm anger you showed when I told you to rid yourself of your friend—it *doesn't* appear that you've been freed from your bindings, not at all."

"What...?"

"You should be seething with all of hell's fury after I tried to rile you up with that 'erasing your friend' nonsense. Your interpretation... No, the choice you made, I should say, was wrong." Tamaki pushed his sunglasses up with a finger and his lips formed a cruel, twisted smile. "You can't express your emotions well in the least, and you're no longer an exorcist. What value do you have? Is your story even progressing as it should?"

"I-I..."

He was right. I should have been angry. I should have been furious that he'd even suggested erasing my friend. So why...why did I feel nothing inside me? Where was my anger? Where were the emotions that made one human?

Was I really human...?

"That's enough, Tamaki!" somebody cut in.

Tamaki looked to see who it was and shrugged in defeat. It was Yao Bikuni, her beautiful face surging with anger and glaring straight at him.

Tamaki let out a deep sigh and turned on his heel. "I suppose I stuck my nose too far where it didn't belong... Oh, young man, if you ever truly find yourself no longer needing that Inugami, come find me. As a story-seller, I'll teach you what you want to know. Kindness is one of my selling points, you see."

He left, leaving nothing but those unsettling words behind. I watched him go, still confused. My heart felt nothing. My body was rooted to the spot.

"You said you were Suimei, from the apothecary, right?

Goodness, you're as white as a sheet." Yao Bikuni was visibly irritated as she scratched her face along the edge of her hood. With some reluctance, she said, "Oh, what to do... You look so unsettling like that, as pale as a doll. Fine. I have a job for you. Look after a soul for me."

Unable to think a thing, I slowly met her gaze.

"You're just the man for the job as you are now. Will you accept it?"

Her beautiful face stared back at me with displeasure—her eyes full of contempt.

Drip. Drip. The sound of water slowly trickling could be heard somewhere near. I walked down the hallway, the floor creaking under my bare feet, and took a casual glance out the window. A large, red fish swam close, nearly touching the windowpane. The fish—I didn't know its name—glared at me with its round eyes before paddling its tail and quickly swimming past. I turned forward again and let my eyes drop down to the glimmerfly flapping in its paper lantern.

I was in the submerged building at the bottom of the lake. As strange as it was, the building was filled with air, so I had no fear of drowning. Zashiki cells lined the sides of the hallway, from which came countless human groans, and screams, and sobs. I felt eyes watching me from here and there as I silently made my way along.

Plip. Every now and then, a bubble formed and rose to the surface of the lake. Every time I heard it, I imagined what would happen if the air suddenly disappeared, and discomfort tugged at me.

"Good morning." Before long, I reached a lacquered, vermilion lattice grid door. A single nun stood before it. She wore a veil typically used in Shinto rituals that hid her face, as all the nuns who looked after those living in these zashiki cells did. I wondered if such a thing had any meaning.

The nun opened the lattice grid door and said the usual. "Please refrain from using light beyond this point, and do not grow closer than necessary with those imprisoned here. Of course, you are expressly forbidden from giving your own name, as well as from asking for others' names."

"I know."

"Take care to not forget..."

I handed the paper lantern to the nun and set foot inside. Beyond this point was a prison of stone, carved out from the island's base. Not a single ray of sunlight penetrated its darkness, but tight bundles of moss glowed on the ceiling, making it possible to see once one's eyes adjusted. Along both sides of the cold, stone passageway were more wooden lattice grid walls. Most of the prisons beyond those walls lay silent and empty, as the only souls who stayed here were those with whom the nuns regularly met.

I walked for a few minutes before finally reaching the cell I was looking for. The light of the ceiling moss didn't reach the back of the cell. I couldn't make out anything within it, as though it had been painted from top to bottom with black ink.

Once I approached, a woman's voice spoke to me. "...Hello, hello. You came again, I see." Her pale hand extended out from the prison, and she beckoned me to hurry. Her arm was so thin and white, it looked as though no blood flowed through the veins visible along the surface of her skin. Her long, willowy fingers seemed feminine, as did the small palm they extended from.

I gave the medicine and book I was carrying to the hand, then told her the book's title. The hand slunk back into the darkness of the cell.

"Oh... How nostalgic," she giggled. Just when I thought she would begin turning the book's pages, she began reciting it from memory instead. Her soft voice echoed throughout the stone prison. I listened and slowly closed my eyes. The time I spent with her always felt peaceful, even if I had only three days for reference.

The request Yao Bikuni had given me was to help a particular soul. The nun prepared ten picture books, ones meant less for children and more for mothers to read to infants, for me to give to the soul, one by one, over the course of ten days. She also requested that I bring some medicine mixed at the apothecary.

I felt that the reward Yao Bikuni had offered was way too much for the level of work. Of course, I had made sure to tell Noname about this arrangement. Ten days was by no means a short time span, so I figured she would be a little put off by the idea. Surprisingly, however, she readily agreed to it.

*"Go ahead and take those ten days off. Now that you've accepted it, you better see this request through in its entirety."*

All I had to do was deliver books and medicine. Did it get any easier than that? I decided to use these ten days to rest from all the sleepless nights I had been having.

"I used to have a kid, you know," the woman said. "Before he was born, I worried myself sick over whether or not I could be a parent. But the moment he was born and I saw my cute little monkey, I laughed. I just understood it instinctually. This was my child."

"...I see."

She told me about her child whenever I gave her a book, speaking with a gentle warmth that I couldn't understand.

"Of course, child-rearing was difficult. I had to wake up every two hours to breastfeed. I can't count how many times I wished I could just go back to sleep... But every time I held his soft body in my arms and smelled the milky scent of him suckling, those feelings went away, and I found my purpose again. Can you relate?"

"Not really, no," I answered. "I can't say I've ever been near a baby."

"Oh dear! You're missing out, then. If you ever spot a small child, try and smell them next time."

"I think that'd get me on some sort of list."

"I suppose you're right!" She laughed like a lovely bell. "I used to read this book here right outside the house—so we could listen to the bugs singing. Inside the book was a red circle, a white circle, a round balloon, and a wormy apple. I remember watching my baby's tiny little hands reach out and touch the pictures, full of wonder. To an adult like me, they were just colored circles... But my baby must have seen them differently."

Time seemed to pass slowly when I was with her. Occasionally, I would hear a distant plip as a bubble of air floated up to the lake surface, but other than that, it was just her voice in this dark, stony prison.

*Did my mother love me like this woman loved her child?* Every so often, as I listened, the thought crossed my mind, and misery would creep into me. Mother was gone. I would never see her again. But whenever I thought back to her warmth, I grew distressed—I wanted to cry from the longing. I wanted to see her again. I wanted to hold someone in my arms.

Just what was this emotion called? This ticklish, oppressive, yet impossible-to-live-without emotion. I couldn't have guessed that such a thing existed within me.

With a slight bounce to her voice, the woman said, "Hey. I can't see you, but you're smiling right now, aren't you?"

"What makes you say that?"

"You feel like you just got a tad bit softer."

"Is that so."

I was glad I had taken this job. This total darkness was just what I'd needed to reflect on myself. I needed time to confirm that I could feel anything at all after failing to feel anger back then.

Besides, those strings that always tried to control me couldn't reach me in this dark, deep place. Here, I could be free.

I continued to talk to the unnamed woman in the darkness, desperately trying to prove to myself that I was a human being with emotions.

After parting with the woman, I climbed a ladder connecting the bottom of the lake to the temple above. I pushed open a heavy metal door, arrived outside, and filled my lungs with fresh air as I stared at the sky above.

The sky of the spirit realm was dark, as it always was. A swarm of glimmerflies happily fluttered across it, fully enjoying their freedom.

"Suimei!"

"Kaori..."

Out of nowhere, Kaori appeared and ran up to me. She suggested we walk home together. "I just swung by to deliver some more books. Yao Bikuni told me you would be coming up soon."

"I see."

"Is the job going well?"

"I guess. I just deliver things."

"Ah." Kaori smiled, looking genuinely happy for me. We talked about trifling things as we crossed the bridge connecting the island to shore. The time I spent with Kaori was peaceful, just like the time I spent with that woman.

"Hey, Kaori... Do you remember your own mother?" I asked.

She looked surprised for a moment, then frowned a bit sadly. "Nope. I wandered into the spirit realm before I was really aware of my surroundings."

"I see."

Kaori stopped and looked at me. "Why that question all of a sudden?"

I hesitated for a moment, but I was the one who'd brought the topic up in the first place, so I figured I should say it. "The person I'm bringing the medicine and books to talks about her child a lot. Like...really happily."

"Oh?"

"Listening to her reminds me of my late mother. Whenever that happens, this area here," I pointed to my chest, "begins to ache and feel warm... It's weird. I just can't understand what emotion this is that I'm feeling."

Kaori blinked a few times, then suddenly erupted into laughter while hugging her sides. She wiped the tears away from the corners of her eyes and pompously placed her hands on her hips. "That's love, I tell ya. Love!"

"Love...?"

"Yup. It's a very, very important emotion that lets you treasure someone." Kaori grinned. "Suimei, you loved your mother very much."

"You think so?" I put my hand to my chest. Even now, when I thought of my mother, I felt something warm welling up inside. I loved my mother? Then, did my mother love me back? I cocked my head. "I don't think I can understand this yet..."

"Oh, don't worry about it," she said. "Most people have a hard time telling if they're loved by the people they've been with for a long time. Being loved feels so natural, we forget we are at all.

Nobody wants it to be that way, but it is, and it leads to all kinds of fights and misunderstandings. Kinda weird, isn't it?"

*I see. So love is a complicated thing.*

Kaori turned away and gazed out at the lake. "That's why you have to clearly tell those important to you that you love them. As long as both sides keep reminding one another, neither will forget they love each other. Putting our thoughts into words is important. Feelings are invisible to the eye, after all."

She stretched her arms high and said, "Mmm...aah! I haven't said it lately to Shinonome-san myself. 'Thank you, Father! I want to eat better, so go earn some more money!' and whatnot." She smiled playfully before breaking into a cackle.

I shrugged. "Isn't that a little different?"

"You think so?" Kaori asked before continuing to happily waltz along the bridge.

Was love the kind of emotion that made one's chest warm and achy? I supposed humans—no, *hearts* were more complex than I knew.

"Can I ask you something, Kaori?" Something that still bothered me abruptly surfaced in my mind.

"Whoa. What's up now?"

I grabbed her hand. It was warmer than mine and fit snugly in my grip. It was so soft, I found myself doubting that we could be the same human species. I looked into her eyes. She was three years older than me and, to my slight displeasure, just a bit taller. With great deliberation, I ventured a thought. "When I'm with you, my chest feels weird. Is this...love too?"

"Wh-what?!"

"I'm not sure, but if we go by what you said earlier, that's what it is."

Kaori blushed as red as a tomato and began scanning the area around her. Her hand, held in my own, turned clammy. When I saw this, I became sure that my suspicions were correct.

*I...love—*

But before my mind could finish the thought, Kaori brushed away my hands and began to speak hysterically. "W-wait, I didn't explain well enough! Uh, th-those symptoms could point to a bunch of different things! You're probably, um...feeling admiration toward an elder you respect! Yes, that's it!"

"*You?* An elder I respect?"

"Yeah! That's gotta be it! Or maybe it's a heart or lung problem! Worth visiting a doctor for!" Step by step, Kaori widened the distance between us. Suddenly, she raised a hand in an over-exaggerated manner and said, "W-well, Miss Kaori's special consultation ends here! Adios!"

She turned on her heel and bolted.

I watched her go and thought to myself, *I see. So this feeling in my chest is something else entirely new.*

"Emotions are complicated..." I looked up at the sky and let out a deep sigh.

Morning again. Rain drizzled down and dampened the courtyard. It poured without break, filling the courtyard and its four adjoining rooms with sound as it cleansed the air of its filth.

"Are you going alone again?" Kuro asked with a whine as I prepared my things.

I crouched down and hugged him. "Don't worry. The job's going fine, and lately, the spirits have accepted me as a Strangeling. I can walk around alone without much danger."

"But who knows what might happen? At least let me see you there."

"No. I was told I had to do this job alone."

As I said this, Kuro sadly wagged his tail.

*He really did worry for me...* I buried my face into his warm fur. "I'm not sure why, but I get the feeling that I should do this job alone. I feel like only then can I understand..."

"Understand what?"

"How to feel anger, Kuro."

He tilted his head. My words evidently weren't getting through.

I smiled and put my nose to his. "I want to be able to feel anger when someone mocks or threatens those dear to me."

"Are you still hung up on what happened that one time? I don't mind it at all, you know."

"I know, but... This is something I have to do. So please...wait for me."

Kuro's puppy dog eyes began to moisten, and he licked the tip of my nose. I laughed at the ticklishness, encouraging him to climb onto me and lick my face even more.

"Hey, Kuro, stop it... It tickles!"

"What's wrong? This is how we express our love!"

*Oh. So love can be expressed like this too.* I smiled lightly and hugged him tightly one more time.

"Never a sour moment between you two, is there?" I turned to see Noname standing at my room's entrance. She handed me a bag of medicine. "Here, today's portion."

"Thanks."

She stared intently at me as I took the bag. "Suimei...how have you been sleeping?"

"No change, sadly," I answered.

She reached out and patted my hair. "Bedhead. If...if you ever change your mind and want to try some medicine, let me know. Of course, the best thing would be for you to sleep soundly without aid, but beggars can't be choosers."

"All right..." I felt bad for making her worry, so I added, "Sorry."

With a sad smile, she said, "I hope you can come to trust this world soon."

"You knew?" I looked at her with surprise.

"But of course." Noname shrugged. "Not only were you an exorcist who fought spirits, but you're a human being. I can't imagine you'd be able to trust spirits right away."

"Yes, well..."

"You're different from Kaori, who was raised here. Take your time. I'll wait as long as I must to earn your trust." Noname smiled tenderly and gave me a quick "Good luck with your job," before leaving the room.

Without thinking, I left the room, chasing after her. I opened my mouth to say something, but I just couldn't find the words.

*Trust.*

I was fairly sure that I held that emotion toward Kuro. But how was I supposed to develop it toward others? How was I supposed to know who to feel it for?

Emotions were so complicated... I wished someone could just tell me all the answers.

I clenched my fist and watched Noname leave. A sweet scent tickled my nose—the scent of tea olive. It was a soft fragrance that didn't overwhelm, gentle to its core.

"Aaaaaaaaaaaaaaaagh!"

Today marked the fifth day I visited the woman. At present, she was having one of her occasional sporadic fits of emotion.

"Aaah, my baby!" Her screams echoed throughout the zashiki cell. Listening to her made me painfully aware that, despite how calm she might have looked before, her soul was too damaged to endure reincarnation. She had lingering regrets to do with her child. I could only imagine what wretched fate had befallen her.

Even someone as dull to emotion as me could understand the grief of having something horrible happen to my child. But grief wasn't all the woman felt.

"Why...?! If...if only I could have stayed by your side!" The woman thrashed her body wildly against the walls of the stone prison, causing chunks of stone to fall down. "Why couldn't I protect my child? Why couldn't I make him happy?"

The woman held a fierce anger directed at none other than herself. Whenever it surfaced, she became unable to control herself and began harming her own body. I had been so shocked the first time I saw it that I'd tried to call for help.

But of course, the woman was not alive, so her attempts at self-harm were meaningless. Her body bore no injuries nor felt any pain, a fact she further lamented. After realizing she couldn't atone through self-harm, she would soon after start apologizing to her child.

I could do nothing but watch. I didn't think there was anything I—someone who couldn't understand her circumstances, her sadness, her anger—could say to her without only hurting her more.

"Why...?!" Like on the other days, the woman's wails gradually eased into weeping.

I gripped the book I was supposed to hand her tightly. I wanted to free her from her suffering, even if I could only lessen it by a second. If I were to give the book to her now...would I calm her rage and be able to hear her gentle voice again?

That was what these books were for, right? The last light of salvation for their souls, the spider's thread.

"Oh, my. She's hollering away again, I see." Yao Bikuni suddenly appeared, filling the prison with the stench of tobacco.

I grimaced before approaching her. "...Some days before, you said I was just the man for this job. Why was that? If what keeps driving this woman mad is anger, did you give me this job to try and make me learn it?"

Yao Bikuni blew a puff of tobacco smoke into my face, causing me to choke. She gave me a look of displeasure and curtly replied, "Think for yourself. I am not so kind as to tell you everything."

I coughed. "B-but..."

"But nothing. I am just doing my job. Besides, a person's emotions are theirs alone. You cannot learn them through imitation." She looked down on me, narrowing her eyes into an icy stare. "Think of emotions as a powerful medicine, young man. They can heal, but they can just as easily send one spiraling into an abyss. They cannot be controlled in the slightest. It is thanks to emotions that humans know joy, but those same emotions also drive men to murder."

"What are you trying to say...?"

"If it weren't for those emotions you so desperately desire, this zashiki cell would be empty."

Just then, the woman slammed her body against the lattice grid wall. "Aaaaaaaaaaaagh!"

"How noisy. No matter how much you scream or lament or cry...nothing will change. Don't you realize it's all too late anyhow?" Yao Bikuni looked coldly upon the woman, who writhed in anger and sadness.

I couldn't help but pity the woman. "Don't be stupid; it's not too late. Her soul can still be saved by reading these books. She always calms down when I give them to her."

Yao Bikuni raised an eyebrow at me and scoffed. "Books cannot save this soul."

"What?"

"Be it books or movies or memories, only a small handful can be saved by such things. Oh, how sorrowful. Truly, how sorrowful. Why is this world filled with such sorrow?" Yao Bikuni spoke in her singsong tone, then turned her back to me. "Salvation doesn't come easily. Even if one wishes for it from the depths of their heart, the gods will always have their backs turned."

Something about her figure from behind looked sad. She seemed so small as she was now, covered in black cloth.

"Why...?" I stared at the book in my hand, and my voice burst out in a yell. "If this book won't save her, then why are you making me bring them?!"

"Because if it's at all possible, I want her to be saved..." Yao Bikuni muttered. "Either way, you've been paid. See through your remaining days." She waved and left.

"You think she can't be saved but want me to try anyway? ...I don't understand." I couldn't make sense of her words. My head was pure chaos. I wanted to scream and thrash.

"What's wrong?" Suddenly, I heard the woman's voice. Her fit must have stopped while I wasn't paying attention. As though not remembering her earlier emotional outburst at all, she reached a white hand through the lattice grid wall and beckoned.

I approached and put the medicine and book into her hand like always.

She laughed. "Not that. Or are you against this old lady touching you?"

It appeared she wanted to touch my hand. I hesitated for a moment, but eventually I gingerly put my fingers on hers.

Her hand was absent of warmth, clearly not of the living. It was as cold as the stone walls around us. But something about the smoothness of her pale and willowy fingers comforted me.

Once I touched her, she reached out further and brushed my hand. "You're warm. It's as though I can feel your kindness."

I jerked my hand back and violently shook my head. "I'm not kind. I can't even get properly angry when those important to me are being belittled. How could an emotionless puppet be kind?"

"Puppet?"

"Yes. My father... My family raised me to be emotionless, an easy-to-control puppet."

Ah... My chest ached. I could tell this ache didn't come from love. It made breathing hurt, and it made me wish I could curl up and hug my knees. Kaori was right. This ache could mean many things. Without thinking, I frowned and cast my eyes down.

"Hey, come closer," the woman said.

"Huh?"

"C'mon, closer. Yes, just like that."

I did as she said and leaned against the lattice grid wall. Then, she reached out from the darkness with both arms and hugged me. I froze, taken by surprise.

"It's all right..." she said gently. "Good boy... It must have been hard, having to be a puppet." She moved closer to my ear and whispered. "So what if you have some difficulties expressing emotions? That's completely fine. Did you know, the first thing humans learn to do is cry?"

"Huh?"

"We cry because we're spooked. We cry because we're hungry. We can't help it, because that's just how babies are, you know?" She giggled. "But after that, we learn to smile. At first, our hearts aren't in it. We smile out of simple physiological response. But over time, we learn to mean it. We learn what joy is, and we commit to memory the faces of those we love. We learn to express the feelings overflowing inside us with a smile."

"Really..."

The woman was talking about the stages of infant development. I, who had up until then thought people were just born full of emotion, listened intently.

"The very last thing we learn is anger. By that point, we're no longer babies but toddlers. Toddlers are very moody things, freely angered when things don't go their way. We even call the period out of infancy the 'terrible twos' because of it. It's a very trying period for parents."

I felt the woman hug me tighter through the lattice grid wall and sensed some hesitation.

"You don't need to feel bad about not getting angry; people develop their emotions in order. I know you can smile, and I know you can cry. You simply haven't learned how to get angry yet. I recommend reading lots of books. Books are the best for developing emotions. You have all the time in the world to read. After all..."

*Your life has only just begun.*

Saying that, she began to wrap something around my wrist.

"This is a charm. The black and red beads are beautiful, aren't they? They're my favorite colors. Please, take it. I hope it brings you good fortune in life."

Ah... I felt it again. What did this ache in my chest mean? Why did my lips tremble so?

"What makes you say that…?" I asked.

"Hm?"

"Why do you say my life's only just begun?"

"It's because you're just like a newborn child. You cry, you smile, but you still can't get angry."

"I don't recall ever crying in front of you."

"I don't know about that. I was able to work out that you were smiling from your general feel before, but today's different." The woman gently brushed my head and whispered, "Because I can feel your warm tears on my arm."

I clenched my teeth so she wouldn't hear me sob, and I gently placed my hand over her arm. Her arm was cold, just like her hand, but something about its chill was comforting, so I stayed like that for some time, unmoving.

My peaceful days with the woman quickly neared their end.

As the tenth day approached, I found myself spending more and more time in the prison. I talked about various things with the woman and gave her many different books—not just the ones Yao Bikuni provided but also others I brought from the bookstore.

Now that I thought back on it, nobody had ever actually properly read a book to me before. Perhaps the ones who raised me hadn't considered it necessary, or had even thought it would be detrimental to my obligation to control my emotions.

The woman was the first to ever read a book to me, and so many at that.

She loved picture books the most. She loved how they reminded her of her child and always had happy endings. Children's literature was filled to the brim with the fantastical; it was a world full of impossibilities made easily possible. Their stories always tickled my imagination and moved my heart.

I learned that stories are a conversation between author and reader. Stories convey messages. Sometimes this message conflicts with the reader's beliefs, and sometimes they resonate. For the first time in my life, I understood what it meant to enrich your mind.

Finally, the tenth day came. The last day. On that day, Yao Bikuni instructed me to wait until night to go into the dark. Like always, she didn't explain why—it was always "think for yourself" with her—but I did so anyway, thinking it strange all the while.

*Huh...?*

I had just reached the bank of the lake when I noticed the sky was far brighter than usual. The sky of the spirit realm took on a redder color when autumn came, just as nature's leaves did. But that red was exceedingly more potent than it should have been, overwhelming the light of the stars and casting the earth in crimson.

It unnerved me.

*I have to hurry.*

I hoofed it toward the small island, glancing into the lake as I crossed the bridge. Ripples skirted across the water's surface, concealing the underwater prison from view. I felt some relief at that fact, as while it was never as bad as the first time I'd seen it, something about the sight of that prison remained unsettling to me.

I had been in a melancholic mood the entire day and would have preferred not to deal with the sight of that prison. I wasn't quite sure *why* I felt melancholic, however, as it wasn't any particular anniversary or otherwise special day, other than being the last day of this job.

Finally, I crossed the bridge. All around me on the island, nuns were hurriedly scampering around. At the center of them all was Yao Bikuni, telling the others what to carry and to where. I felt a cold sweat run down my back the moment I realized the nuns were moving *humans*. The humans lay unmoving on stretchers, carried by the nuns, and black cloths covered their heads.

"Oh, you came," Yao Bikuni called.

I twitched before bowing my head to her. Then, like always—no, a bit faster than usual—I made my way to the woman in the prison.

But I was immediately stopped. Just before the vermilion, lacquered lattice grid door I always passed, a veiled nun blocked my way. "The prison is empty today."

"Wha—" I spun around to look at Yao Bikuni and stammered, "Wh-where is she?"

"Who?"

"You know who... The one I've been bringing books to all this time, where is she?!"

She pointed to a rough woven mat onto which the humans were being tumbled, their heads still covered by black cloths. I immediately ran forward and reached for the nearest black cloth I could.

"You mustn't!" Yao Bikuni yelled, making me pause. "...Don't get in the way, you fool."

"How is this getting in the way?"

"It simply is. Just don't do anything and watch. Besides, what good would removing their cloths do? Do you even know what her face looks like?"

She was right. The only thing I knew about the woman was her voice and her hands...

I pulled my hand back. Seeing I had given up, Yao Bikuni looked up at the sky. She appeared to be waiting for something.

"What the hell is going on...?" Unsure what to do, I simply stood where I was. All around me, the nuns still hurried from place to place. I looked into the bag I had brought and saw the books I had planned to give the woman. According to her, these books were a bit different from her usual fare. These were the books she had wanted to read with her child once he grew up.

"That's too bad..." The words spilled out of my mouth before I realized it. Too bad for who? Was she the one looking forward to reading these books together? Or was it me?

Suddenly, I heard a scream.

"Aaah... You mustn't... You mustn't go!"

It came from a nun on her knees before the woven mat. She was holding down one of the black cloths covering a face. I was confused as to what was going on—until I realized the contents of the black cloth were wriggling.

"It's begun," Yao Bikuni said, pointing toward the sky. "The Leonids will be showering today. Each shooting star will coincide with somebody's soul burning out."

*What in the world is this nun saying?* I wondered. I stared at her, confused.

A bit pale-faced, she raised an eyebrow at me. "It's a bit unusual for us to have clueless strangers here on such a sickening day. Then again, I suppose you've been too involved to be a stranger at this point. I guess you have a right to know. I've been in a somber mood today. Maybe telling you might fix that..."

She gazed at the humans lined along the woven mat and continued, "In ancient times, shooting stars were seen as ominous things. *The Records of the Three Kingdoms* even uses a shooting star as the premonition of Zhuge Liang's coming death in the Battle of Wuzhang Plains."

"So what? Isn't that just superstition?"

"Ha ha. You mustn't forget, this isn't the human world. Here in the spirit realm, shooting stars are a true premonition of death... The sky of the spirit realm is terrifying. It shows the moment someone passes away ever so clearly. Weak souls can't mentally handle seeing such things, so we hide them away at the bottom of the lake where it is dark, where they are the farthest possible distance from the sky."

Yao Bikuni looked at the sky with great irritation and clicked her tongue. "But today is one of the few times a year a meteor shower comes near the Earth. We can't stop the meteor showers from whisking away the weaker souls, so we bring them up here. This is their last chance."

*Does someone die every time a shooting star streaks across the sky, or does a shooting star streak across the sky every time someone dies?* That question flared into my mind, but I quickly suppressed it. That wasn't important now. What was important was that today, a great number of souls would disappear.

Yao Bikuni sighed deeply, then yelled at the souls lying on the woven mat. "You've rested enough, haven't you?! Pull yourselves together and get on with your next lives already! You'll be whisked away by the stars at this rate, and then you'll truly fade to nothingness. Please, just move on already."

There was no reply.

She grimaced and muttered, "Today really is a sickening day."

In the next instant, a streak of light dashed across the sky. For a moment, a faint white line remained before fading away—a shooting star. The second it appeared, a dramatic change occurred within a number of the souls. From beneath their black cloth coverings, a dim light leaked. Gradually, those lights grew stronger, until they grew so bright that I couldn't look at them directly. Before long, something fluttered out from underneath one of the black cloths. Its ghostly wings moved gracefully in the air, illuminating its surroundings with a dazzling light.

"A glimmerfly," I murmured. The moment I did so, numerous glimmerflies poured out from underneath the black cloth and took to the skies.

The nuns began to wail.

"Aaah!"

"No, you mustn't!"

The area began to brighten. Alarmed, I quickly looked around and saw more glimmerflies emerging here and there. As they rose, they fluttered about one another playfully, forming clusters. Those various clusters fell into a single line, becoming a miniature Milky Way in the sky, enhanced by the remaining traces of the shooting stars that still hung in the sky.

The wails and cries of the nuns continued. Their tears wet the earth as they lamented the fate of the souls in their care who had refused reincarnation.

As the number of glimmerflies increased, one after another, Yao Bikuni muttered, annoyed. "Glimmerflies are the shadows of souls, emitting their final lights before burning out completely. Ah... Such beautiful yet repulsive bugs they are. It truly confounds me that they long to be near humans, when they've rejected a new life of their own."

The revelation of the glimmerflies' true nature hit me like a truck. But that wasn't what was important right now.

*What do I do?*

A panic began to rise in me. That woman was out here too, and at this rate, she would become glimmerflies as well. But how could I find someone whose name and face I didn't know?

As my mind raced, more and more glimmerflies were born and began their journey to the sky.

"Suimei?" I heard a familiar voice behind me.

"Ah..." Feeling like I was about to cry, I slowly turned around. Standing there was my little partner, Kuro. "Why are you here?"

"Yao Bi... Bi...? Er, that nun sent me a letter saying that today was a special day and you would need help."

Shocked, I looked at Yao Bikuni. She was comforting a crying nun by gently patting her back.

"I don't really get what's going on, but do you need help, Suimei? Maybe I could help you?" Kuro asked, looking up at me with his puppy dog eyes.

*Hah. That nun is kinder than she claims.* I grinned wryly and crouched down. "Please help me. There's someone I want you to find, Kuro."

I took an item from my pocket: a string of black and red prayer beads. They were the only thing I had received from that woman, a beautiful charm meant for my good fortune. With its smell, we might be able to find her.

Understanding my intent, Kuro quickly smelled it but immediately froze afterward.

"Kuro?"

He slowly looked up at me. "...Suimei, just who have you been seeing?"

"What?"

He then bolted off as quickly as he could.

"Kuro, wait!"

He ignored me, speeding away like a bullet, until he stopped before a soul. I struggled to catch up, only to find Kuro stiff as a board.

"Kuro? What's wrong?"

"Suimei..." He looked up at me. "What is Midori doing here?"

"Mo...ther?"

Midori was my mother's name.

*You must be strong. Any time you feel lonely, or like you might lose control of yourself, just pull Inugami close and sleep.* Those were the last words she had left me with before she died when I was five.

"Midori. Midori. Wake up. Midori!" Kuro frantically tried to shake awake the soul who he claimed was my mother. But the soul didn't respond.

"Ah, jeez! Always the late riser, aren't you?!" Impatient, Kuro bit the black cloth covering the soul and flung it off—revealing a terribly thin woman.

My mind froze the moment I saw her. The mother in my memories had luxurious black hair and a beautiful, albeit pale, face. I could clearly recall her gentle light-brown eyes even now. But the woman before me was different. Her face was gaunt, and her hair was gray. Her lips were cracked dry and her eyes sunken. She was so thin that her collarbone was clearly outlined through her white robe. She looked like she could wither to dust at any moment.

Was this my mother? *Her?*

The inside of my head felt like a mess. My beautiful mother. My beloved mother. The mother who warmed me in her embrace. The mother who accepted everything about me and could do anything... Could this weak woman really be her?

Suddenly, the woman faintly opened her eyes and, with great effort, began to speak. "Is...is this a dream? I see Kuro here..."

"Midori! It's not a dream. I'm here. I'm really here with you!" Kuro said.

"Ha ha. You sound so energetic, Kuro. And you're just as cute as ever," she said before breaking into a coughing fit. After some deep breaths, she smiled and continued. "I'm so happy I could meet you at the end of my life as a soul..."

Gently, she closed her eyes.

There was no mistaking it. It was her. This woman was my mother after all.

The moment I realized that, my chest began to tighten so badly that it hurt to breathe. I fell to my knees and held my chest. A wave of nausea overcame me, and I broke out in a cold sweat. My vision became blurry and my balance unstable. The world spun around me, and my body no longer did as I wanted.

"S-Suimei?! Are you okay?!" Kuro ran up to me.

With a trembling hand, I reached out and touched his small body. The moment I felt his soft warmth, I calmed down a bit. But my head was still filled with questions.

*Why? Why? Why? Why? Why—why would Mother refuse to reincarnate?*

"Sui...mei?" my mother mumbled, having heard Kuro.

Timidly, I looked at her as she lay on her side. She turned her head to face me and opened her eyelids the narrowest bit, revealing eyes that were a light brown that matched mine. They looked just as I remembered them.

"Is my sweet little baby really here?"

"Ah..." I looked down at my body in shock. Perhaps my mother still believed that I was five years old. I cursed myself for having grown. Of course, there wasn't anything I could have done to prevent it, but I cursed myself nonetheless for not having the exact appearance that my mother was looking for.

*If I said I was her son, wouldn't she be disappointed?* That thought only lasted for a fleeting moment as Kuro, with his tail standing taut and his pink tongue hanging out, said in his happy-go-lucky voice, "He is, he is! Suimei's right here, Midori!"

*Oh, Kuro, you simpleminded idiot...* I frowned and met my mother's eyes.

She stared at me unblinkingly for a while, before abruptly her face crinkled into a smile. "My... You've grown into a fine young man."

She then spread her arms wide. I froze, not understanding her intent for a moment, but soon I realized that my mother was looking for a hug. I moved closer.

"Moth...er?" I crouched beside her. Too embarrassed to hug her, I touched her hands. Ah... They were the same hands I'd felt in the prison. Cold and willowy, yet soft. Her hand gently brushed my cheek. She was gentle, so gentle, like she was touching a treasure. "Mother..."

"I can't believe it. It's a miracle. You're really here, Suimei..."

"Mother..."

"You've grown so big. I'm sorry I didn't recognize you earlier. I never realized it was you bringing me those books. But then again, it was so dark, wasn't it?"

"Mother...!" I didn't know what to say, what to talk about. All I could do was say "Mother, Mother," over and over like a broken record.

The corner of her eyes creased as she smiled. Transparent droplets dribbled out of her eyes as she gazed at me lovingly. That was when she said something strange. "I have no more regrets. Now I can fade away with my heart at ease."

My eyes grew wide. "Wh-why? How could you want to fade away? I don't understand..."

"Ha ha. It's simple, my child..." Her lids lowered, and she spoke sadly. "I've made you unhappy. That is my sin. Nothing more, and nothing less. I'm a mother who failed to protect her child. I'm a mother who caused pain to her child. I'm a mother who couldn't be there for her child. Those reasons alone are more than enough to refuse my next life."

She reached out and touched my white hair. Tears fell from her eyes yet again. "It must have been so difficult...so painful... to believe you were a puppet. I'm so, so sorry..." She looked me straight in the eyes and continued to apologize. "I had the choice of not bearing you. No matter how you looked at it, you couldn't have been happy in that house. But I bore you anyway, just because I wanted to have a cute baby. That was the only thing on my mind. You're a victim, Suimei. A victim of my own human ego. Won't you hate this foolish mother of yours?"

The hand brushing my hair stopped and fell. I watched, aghast, as gravity pulled it down—but before it could fall completely,

I caught it in my hand. She blinked a few times and looked at me in surprise.

With certainty, I felt it.

I was loved.

I was loved by my mother from the bottom of her heart.

As though the sun had come to dwell in my chest, warmth began to spread throughout my body. All the stories I had heard in that zashiki prison had been about *me*. All the words she had offered for her precious, beloved child, those had been for me!

In this moment, I felt nothing but proud to call this woman, who put her child before herself, my mother. I felt that I too could put her before all else. She was precious to me, irreplaceable.

*Ah... Is this... Is this what* love *is?*

Finally placing a name to the emotion welling up inside me, I reached out to my mother, lifted her up, and hugged her feeble body. I hugged her tightly, as though trying to make certain she was, indeed, with me in that moment. I thought about what she meant to me and said, "...I still remember you. Your warmth. The smile you would only briefly show. Your gentle smell. Yes, there were many struggles in my life, but I always had my memories of you to get me through them."

I lightened my grip around her and met her shocked gaze. "So please, don't say you've sinned. Don't regret this. Please...don't speak ill of the mother I love. To me, your existence is irreplaceable."

"Suimei..."

"Sure, I may have had some rough patches. I still have some memories that hurt to recall. But now, I am surrounded by friends."

My partner, Kuro. The annoying but helpful Kaori. The nosy Noname. The teasing twins, Kinme and Ginme. The open-minded man who had let me stay at his bookstore, Shinonome.

I didn't have to hunt spirits anymore either. I no longer had to put myself in harm's way, and instead I made my living working at the apothecary. I was living the most peaceful days of my life yet.

"I'm...probably the happiest I've ever been right now. So please... Please..." My throat stung. For some reason, I couldn't speak well. But I had to say it anyway. Kaori was right. We have to clearly communicate our feelings. At this rate, I would be parting with my mother with misunderstandings still left between us. I couldn't allow that to happen!

"I want you to be reborn," I begged her. "Don't disappear, please. Please listen to your child's selfish desire, Mother."

She went wide-eyed for a moment, then relaxed into a soft smile. "...If I'm reborn, maybe I can meet you again. That would be nice."

"Me too!" Kuro said. "I want to meet you too!"

"My! Ha ha, then I guess we all feel the same way."

Kuro stood up on his hind legs and flailed his arms to try and appeal to Mother. She laughed happily from the bottom of her heart as he did. I watched the two talk with a thin smile, but our time together was fast approaching its end.

Without warning, my mother's eyes suddenly became vacant. The strength slipped from her body, and she grew heavy in my arms. Staring up at the sky, she said, "Suimei... I wish I could've read more books to you. I wanted to share more stories with you, and to laugh and cry and be angry together. Live free. Do what you want to do. Don't suppress your emotions anymore. Be true to yourself."

"Mother? What's wrong? You sound like you're making your last requests."

"Perhaps I am... Suimei, if things ever become unbearable, just pull Inugami close and sleep. And if at all possible, find someone who will hold you tight." A single large teardrop fell from her eye. It fell onto my hand, warm.

"Mothe..." I began, but I couldn't finish before her body began to unravel. I watched, mouth agape, as her body came apart like ribbons, starting with her extremities. The pieces that came undone changed shape into butterflies that took to the skies.

"No... Don't go, Mother! Wait!" Like a child, I shouted, reaching for the butterflies flying away. But the graceful butterflies evaded my fingers.

In an instant, an emotion buried deep inside me burst forth. Like magma flowing from a crater, it swallowed me whole and reforged me with incandescent white flames. The insides of my head grew numb, preventing me from thinking anything. I took those flames and directed them at myself, cursing myself over and over for my powerlessness.

"Damn it, no! You can't leave me!" I watched as her body gradually whittled away, becoming lighter and lighter. I could do nothing for her but yell. "No, no, no, you can't leave me! I love you! I love you, damn it! Aaaaaaaaah!"

At that moment, my mother was completely reduced to a

flock of butterflies. The body I held disappeared in its entirety, replaced by the light-scattering butterflies now scrambling toward the sky.

I looked at my hands in a daze. I couldn't do a single thing. My heated mind was quickly cooled by the feeling of loss inside me.

"Ah..." I murmured, noticing there was something left in my hand: a tiny, tiny embryo. Wrapped in golden light, it drew in its undeveloped legs and closed its eyes. Then it floated up into the air and slowly ascended, away into the sky.

"I guess even pigs fly sometimes." While I was stuck in a daze, Yao Bikuni had appeared by my side with a delighted smile.

"What...happened to my mother?" I fearfully asked.

She grinned meaningfully. "Think about it yourself. I'm not so kind as to tell you everything."

"Right..." I released the tension in my body, lay flat on my back, and looked up at the sky. Countless glimmerflies fluttered about. They made flocks and formed a long belt stretching up to the sky, a sight I might have considered beautiful if I weren't aware of their origin. But I *was* aware of their origin, and it made me feel conflicted.

Yao Bikuni, who had begun walking away, stopped and turned around to say, "Oh, right. Keep the truth of these butterflies a secret from Kaori, okay?"

"Why?" I asked.

She raised an eyebrow. "That human girl has no need to know. These butterflies can just remain butterflies to her. Beautiful butterflies that light up the darkness of the spirit realm. If you're a man, you can show that much consideration, right?"

"Fine." I nodded, agreeing to keep the secret. Just as she turned away, self-satisfied, I said, "You're a kind person."

"Huh?! Don't be ridiculous!" she exclaimed.

I smiled at her mortification. "Thank you for letting me meet my mother."

She frowned and turned away with a huff. "I just so happened to be in the mood for a miracle... Congratulations." With that, she left.

"Suimei?" Kaori had appeared in Yao Bikuni's place. She seemed flustered by how different the island was from usual and timidly asked, "Did something happen? Noname told me I should come, but is something going on?"

I really was surrounded by kind people.

With a wry grin, I carefully stood up. I looked up at the blinding number of glimmerflies fluttering away and frowned. "Let's head home."

"Huh? Ah... Sure."

I began to walk toward the bridge when I felt something tug on my sleeve. I turned back to see Kaori with a slightly torn look on her face. "What's up?" I asked.

"Um, well...I'm not really sure what to say, but..." She seemed to hesitate for a moment before making her mind up and spreading out her arms. "It's okay to cry when you feel like crying."

"What...?"

"Remember that time with Sasuke and Hatsu? I felt like my heart had split in two, but I tried not to cry. That was until you said, 'There's nothing wrong with being sad, with feeling lonely, with feeling pain at saying goodbye.'" She drew closer and hesitantly hugged me. "I can tell that you're sad right now, so let me say it this time... 'Just let go and cry...dummy.'"

Ah... My heart ached so painfully... But it was a bittersweet, uplifting ache. Tears naturally welled up in my eyes as I, still a bit uncertain, slowly wrapped my arms around her in a hug.

"You tried your best, Suimei. There, there."

"...Don't treat me like a child, you idiot."

"Sorry!"

I buried my face in her shoulder, trying to muffle my voice as I cried.

Her body warmth permeated my skin, melting the ice in the depths of my heart and cutting the strings that bound my hands and feet.

By the time my tears came to a stop underneath the bright glimmerfly-lit autumn sky, my heart was freer than before.

# CHAPTER 3

# The Hidden House on Tono Mountain

"**O**H? Now just where did you get in from?"

A single glimmerfly fluttered about the room. Perhaps a window had been left open somewhere.

The lost butterfly scattered its phosphorescent light wildly, ignoring my presence. I thought it beautiful—fleeting and phantasmal as it was. I could have stared for all eternity and never grown tired of it.

The butterfly came to rest on my finger, and I smiled. "Would you like to eat too? ...Oh, right. I guess you can't."

I watched as it fluttered away and grinned wryly at myself, then looked down at the steaming-hot baked sweet potatoes on the low table of the living room.

Baked sweet potato, one of autumn's many seasonal treats. In the human world, stalls selling these would pop up throughout towns the moment things became the slightest bit chilly. Such stalls were characteristic of the season itself.

In terms of outer appearance alone, baked sweet potato was unassuming. It wasn't until you peeled away its skin and revealed the luxuriously fluffy golden goodness inside that it took your breath away. Reminiscent of the fields during harvest season, baked sweet potatoes were sweet enough to make one suspect sugar was somehow added inside. You could easily keep snacking away, well aware you were spoiling your dinner as you carelessly reached out for another.

Here too in the spirit realm, baked sweet potato stalls popped up once autumn came. They were managed as a side business by Azuki-arai spirits, spirits that washed beans near rivers and waited for people to fall in. Typically, the Azuki-arai spirits sold azuki beans, but once autumn rolled around, they started selling baked sweet potatoes too.

Once the Azuki-arai began to sing, "Will I grind my azuki beans, or will I find a person to eat?"—an old song they were known to sing in folktales—all the spirits grabbed their wallets and rushed out their doors. The streets flooded with throngs of people at these times, all crowded around the stalls with eager smiles. Not even spirits could resist the scrumptious sugary smell of sweet potatoes being baked.

Of course, I wasn't exempt from the sweet potato's allure either and had lined up the instant I heard the Azuki-arai's song. I bought a large and a small one, but needed something to drink to help me eat the dry, heavy meal. So, I prepared some green tea, as the bitter taste would pair well with the sweetness of the sweet potatoes. Making the tea was a simple matter, as the teapot and cups were already set out and only needed hot water.

The tempting smell of sweet potato filled the room, making me want to dig in that very moment. But I didn't. The man I planned to eat with, Shinonome-san, was not home yet.

"He said he'd be back today..." I shot a look up at the clock on the wall. Shinonome-san had abruptly left three days ago, saying he would be home this day.

I sighed. The paper bag holding the baked sweet potatoes was starting to get soggy from moisture.

*I had the Azuki-arai pick out the best ones for me, and now they're going to be all mushy...*

Feeling gloomy, I put my chin on the low dining table and went slack.

Tick. Tock. Tick. Tock. The ticking of the clock echoed throughout the room. There were no customers in the bookstore, and Nyaa-san had gone off somewhere to play. The ever-bustling house seemed almost alien in its present silence.

I heard children playing in the distance. Not wanting to listen, I got up and tried to distract myself. I hobbled around the room aimlessly in search of something to do, before eventually peering into Shinonome-san's room. Normally, I saw him from behind, locked in battle with his manuscripts, but right now, the only thing at his desk was a well-flattened sitting cushion.

I sighed again. It wasn't unusual for my adoptive father to leave home on a whim for days at a time, but he'd been absent for oddly long and frequent stretches of time of late. I couldn't recall if we had sat down and talked even a single time in the past month.

*What could he be doing? Is it something he can't tell me about?*

Just as that thought crossed my mind, I heard the sliding door open.

"Shinonome-san?" I spun around to look. But once I realized the one standing there wasn't him, I let my shoulders droop. "...Oh, it's just you, Suimei..."

"Is that a problem...?" Standing by the door connecting the bookshop to the living space was Suimei. He narrowed his light-brown eyes with displeasure, then walked in like he lived here. "Today too?"

"Yup..." I gave him the same answer I've given him each time the past few days.

Suimei took one of the sitting cushions from the corner of the room, folded it in half, and lay down, using it as a pillow—as he had done many times recently.

"Want something to drink?" I asked.

He didn't respond.

"Hello? Earth to Suimei-kuuun?"

He still didn't respond. I sneaked a glance at his face and noticed that I could hear him snoozing quietly. A smile burst out of me—I was amazed that he could fall asleep so quickly—and I brought him a blanket.

Ever since he'd finished the job Yao Bikuni gave him, Suimei had occasionally come over to my house to sleep. I didn't know why he did this, but he had said something about wanting to get used to sleeping in a place where he was comfortable to start. I'd told Noname about all this, but she'd just said, "Take care of him," and, "He's trying to come to terms with this world in his own way," her smile gentle.

I prodded Suimei's body with a finger. "So...are you finally starting to warm up to us?" He didn't respond, being already sound asleep.

Suddenly, the events of a few days back came to mind, and I blushed. The sky had been oddly bright then. Thinking back on it, I often saw Noname and Shinonome-san together on such days. Anyway, Noname had asked me to go see Suimei after I visited her apothecary for dinner. I'd found him on the small island as a massive swarm of glimmerflies was fluttering about.

Something had been strange about the island that day. The nuns that worked there were crying, and there were far more glimmerflies than usual. The glimmerflies also seemed to be gathered around the nuns, even though as far as I knew, the insects were only ever drawn to humans.

While I was wondering what was going on, I noticed Suimei talking to Yao Bikuni and called out to him. But the moment I saw his face, I thought my heart might implode. It was as though I were looking at my past self, the one from that summer day, surrounded by the summer cries of the cicada, who had just held two friends as they passed away in her arms. I'd wanted to cry so badly then, but I had been unable to. A strange warmth had smoldered inside me, my emotions wanting to explode but having no outlet by which to do so. It had hurt so much that I had stopped breathing. I never wanted to experience such a thing again.

Suimei's face in that moment was exactly the same as the one I had made then. I didn't know what had happened to him, but I couldn't just do nothing. The words were out my mouth before I knew it: "Let me say it this time... 'Just let go and cry...dummy.'"

I moved on impulse and hugged him. I just couldn't stand not doing so. I wanted to comfort his heart just like he had comforted mine.

Ba-dum, ba-dum. As he trembled, letting his warm tears fall, I wondered—was that pounding heart I heard his or mine?

"Ah, my face feels so warm..." I tried to fan my sweaty face with my hands and thought back to what had happened afterward. After he stopped crying, he had explained a bit about what happened.

"I met my mother," was all he said, but that was enough. I knew that lake was a place where injured human souls gathered. His mother must have been one of those souls, and Yao Bikuni must have brought the two together.

I watched as Suimei slept peacefully now, his chest slowly rising and falling with each breath. With his eyes closed, I could clearly make out the length of his eyelashes. He had the handsome features of a prince, straight out of a fairy tale. I imagine he would've lived a very different life if he weren't born into a line of exorcists.

"It must have been tough," I murmured. From the bottom of my heart, I hoped Suimei could live a life happier than any other.

One to make up for all the pain he had endured...a hundred, no, a thousand times over. Yes, for example, a life where he could make a family with someone he truly loved...

I halted that train of thought the moment it crossed my mind and recalled Suimei's earlier words: *"When I'm with you, my chest feels weird."*

"Aaaahhh! N-nonononono!" I shook my head vigorously, trying to shake the memory away. I hugged my knees and shut my eyes to try and calm down, but my mind wouldn't stop racing. "Ugh... What in the world's going on?"

I let out a grand sigh and then looked toward the shop. "...Shinonome-san, just where could you be?"

I wanted to meet that adoptive father of mine right this instant so I could ask him just what these chaotic feelings inside of me were. Why was he never around when I needed him...? Even though he never left me alone when I *didn't* need him.

It felt like it had been an eternity since I had chatted with him. We only ever made meaningless small talk, but even that was dearly missed.

"I'm definitely going to chew him out once he gets home." I pouted my lips as I strained my ears so I wouldn't miss the sound of the sliding door being opened.

But in the end, Shinonome-san never did come home that day, and the baked sweet potatoes on the table went cold.

The next day came. I had just met up with Nyaa-san in the spirit realm after finishing my part-time job in the human world.

"Is Shinonome-san back?!"

"And hello to you too, Kaori." Nyaa-san wagged her three tails and narrowed her mismatched sky-blue and gold eyes. "He's back."

"Wait, really?! You're not lying to me, are you?"

"Would I lie to you?"

"Uh, if the past is any indication, yes."

"Humph. You got me there." She spun around and lowered herself. "Want to ride me over?"

"Really?!"

"I'm in the mood to see you scold your father. Nobody hurts my best friend and gets away with it." Nyaa-san's body then expanded before my eyes. Her muscles and bones creaked as she grew from an ordinary cat to a massive, nimble, tiger-like beast.

I drove my face into her soft black fur. "I love you, Nyaa-san!"

"Yeah, yeah, let's just get going."

"I even love that callousness of yours!"

"Oh, give me a break."

I hopped onto her back and held on as tight as I could. She took off at a blinding speed, weaving between the spirits coming and going. The scenery shot by, and even the glimmerflies that normally swarmed me trailed far, far behind. The spirits who noticed us coming stepped out of the way, allowing Nyaa-san to continue without slowing down. Spirits doing far crazier things was nothing out of the ordinary here in the spirit realm, so nobody so much as batted an eye at us.

"Are you not stopping by today, Miss Strangeling?" called out the fish dealer I always visited. He was a type of Kappa spirit called Hyosube, from the mountain regions of Miyazaki and Kumamoto.

Taking care not to fall off, I turned toward the Hyosube and yelled, "Sorry! No time!"

"Oh, gotcha! Swing by later then! I got some nice freshwater fish in, hi hi hi!" he said with the characteristic strange Hyosube laugh. The fish at his shop were always varied and plentiful. I was a regular enough customer that he always had what I wanted ready before I walked up.

I waved goodbye to him and promised to swing by later.

"Why not stop by, Kaori-chan?" Noppera-bo called.

"We got some new autumnal sweets in!" his wife called as well. "You should come take a look too, Nyaa-san!"

"We will! Just not now!" I said, taking care not to bite my tongue. Similar exchanges continued until we reached the bookstore.

Too eager to wait for Nyaa-san to come to a complete stop, I leapt off her, stumbled a bit, and then flung the door open. I saw a shadow on the floor of the old, dingy shop and called, "Shinonome-san?!"

The owner of the shadow stepped out from behind a bookshelf and said, "Oh, Kaori." He scratched his stubble and smiled. "It's been a while."

"You're back..." My anger deflated like a balloon the moment I saw his smile, instead replaced by pure joy. I was simply glad to have him back.

That didn't mean I wasn't going to chew him out, of course.

I approached, fully intent on giving him an earful, when my toes bumped into something. I looked down to see piles of books lying on the floor.

"Oh, sorry. I've left a mess." He stared at the shop's book-lending ledger with a deathly serious look on his face, scribbling something with a brush.

Curious, I looked over his shoulder. On the ledger were the titles of many books in one column and his name all along the borrower column. "Are you taking those books somewhere?" I asked.

"Mm-hmm. Need 'em for a bit." He didn't so much as glance up at me as he compared the title on the ledger with the books lying around.

"I see..." Seeing nothing better to do, I decided to put away my things. Normally, I would have then started to bring in the laundry and get dinner ready, but...today I wanted to be with Shinonome-san as much as possible.

Come to think of it, Noppera-bo's wife had said they had those new sweets. She and Noppera-bo ran the best confectionery in the spirit realm, and right around now was the time special sweets made with autumnal fruits started to appear.

*It* is *around snack time right now... Maybe I should go buy some sweets for us to eat?* I got a bit excited at the thought and rushed to grab my wallet. I opened the door connecting the living space to the shop but froze upon seeing my father.

"Hup, and up we go." He lifted a large cloth bundle onto his back, within which I could make out the outline of a large volume of books. In his hands, he carried a timeworn travel bag that didn't pair well with his Japanese clothes. The travel bag, the leather of which was cracking from lack of care, had been a favorite of his for years. It was stuffed to the brim and even had a paper umbrella tied to the handle. He was clearly going somewhere.

"Oh..." I quietly mumbled.

That got his attention. His gray eyes smiled a bit. He then walked up to me and roughly tousled my hair. "I'll be heading out for a few days again. You can go ahead and close the shop on the days you've got your part-time job."

I didn't say anything back.

"Sorry I've been leaving the shop in your hands so much lately. I'll make it up to you, promise."

The smell of tobacco and body odor tickled my nose, a harsh scent that I had grown fond of over the years.

Saying nothing further, he patted my head twice and left the shop.

Thunk. The sound of a sliding door closing echoed throughout the empty bookstore.

"So that's why you've come here, then." Noname looked at me with some astonishment.

On the table at the center of the flowery courtyard were a few hot and steaming meals. We had salt-grilled sweetfish that had been caught by traditional sweetfish traps as they traveled to the mouth of an estuary to lay eggs; glistening fresh white rice, picked just this year and cooked in an earthenware pot; pickled eggplant; rolled omelet—Noname's specialty; and a hearty miso soup. For dessert, we had Noppera-bo's wife's persimmon yokan. Each and every item looked absolutely delicious, and yet...

"Shinonome-san's a dummy..." Because of my bad mood, I couldn't work up an appetite, despite the smorgasbord of autumnal flavors laid out before me.

Nyaa-san, who was busying herself with sniffing a grilled fish, said, "I can't believe you still took the time to stop by the neighbors to shop. You should've just come straight here like I said."

"Well, I promised I would stop by, and you can't break promises..."

"Didn't the one who taught you that break their promise to you?"

I frowned at that.

Nyaa-san drew closer to the still hot grilled fish and said, "Well, whatever. You came here because you didn't want to cook dinner yourself, right?"

"Yeah... I don't feel like doing anything right now. Sorry, Noname."

"I don't mind one bit," Noname said with a smile as she placed a pumpkin gratin on the table. "In fact, I'm glad to be of help. But I'd be sad if there were any leftovers after I worked so hard to cook everything, so try your best to eat up, okay?"

"...Okay." I began with the sweetfish, coated in so much salt that it was nearly pure white. I held it by the skewer and took a huge bite of the midsection, the strong kick of the salt and the bitter taste of fish liver soon spreading inside my mouth. The texture was soft and flaky, and the fish wasn't big but still filling.

The best part was the bitterness of the fish liver. It wasn't the icky kind of bitterness but the kind that had a hidden savory-sweetness hidden within.

Enamored by the taste, I closed my eyes and smiled.

*"Wa ha ha! The Hyosube can nab a good fish, all right. This would pair well with a nice, stiff drink."*

My mind wandered as I imagined what Shinonome-san would say if he were here.

"Ah, jeez!" I exclaimed. *He's the worst!*

"Oh, my..." Noname smiled sadly. "You know what, don't force yourself to eat today, dear. Take it easy."

"You really want to be with that father of yours..." Suimei said, entering the courtyard with a pot in his hands.

"Something wrong with that?" I grumbled, resting my chin on my hands.

Kuro came running up from behind Suimei and said, "I think it's great! Shinonome's a nice dad. A far better dad than this other guy I know, at least... So yeah, nothing wrong with it, Kaori!" He then saw Nyaa-san and let out a surprised yelp, earning a glare from her.

Swaying her tails in the air with a mean look on her face, she silently approached Kuro as though closing in on prey. "...What's wrong? Are you scared of me?"

"Wh-what? There's no way I'd be scared of a cat!"

"Hmm..." She stopped in front of him and put a paw on his snout. He whined fearfully, after which she said, "I guess a mutt will never be anything more than a mutt."

"What in the world are you two doing?" Suimei asked incredulously. He let out an exasperated sigh and began preparing tea. "Anyway, Kaori, it's not that I think there's anything wrong with it, it's just that people your age normally put more distance between themselves and their fathers."

Unlike with Japanese tea, Chinese tea involved a lot of steps. Even so, Suimei prepared the tea with a practiced hand, proof of how used he was to living here.

"What's 'normal' anyway?" I grumbled.

"Hmm, dunno. I haven't really lived a normal life myself," he said as he put a cup of tea in front of me. The smell was so good, I couldn't refrain from peering inside.

"It's qing cha," he said. "Also known as oolong tea. It's good for calming down and helps give you an appetite."

"Really? It's completely different from the oolong tea I know. It smells so much stronger and more refreshing."

"Don't compare this to the cheap stuff. I'm using actual quality tea leaves."

Feeling impressed, I took a sip. The warm and fragrant tea passed through me, and I let out a satisfied sigh. I really did feel calmer. "...It's delicious. Thank you, Suimei."

"Humph." He turned away.

I smiled at his embarrassment, then bowed slightly to him and Noname. "Thanks for trying to make me feel better, both of you. I let myself get too emotional over something so insignificant."

"Oh, Kaori..." Noname, sitting in the chair next to me, frowned. "Don't say that. We all know how important that dimwit is to you."

"Sorry..." I watched the small ripples on the surface of my tea and said, "I...can't help but think the reason Shinonome-san won't tell me where he's going is because I'm not his real daughter."

"His real daughter?" she asked.

"Yeah... You know...because we're not blood relations."

Becoming Shinonome-san's real daughter had been a dream of mine since I was a child. Of course, I was an adult now, and I'd learned a long time ago that such a thing wasn't actually possible. I couldn't cling to such childish fantasies anymore.

Whatever Shinonome-san was doing now was important to him, important enough that he didn't want others to interfere. That was why he couldn't tell anyone except those he truly trusted. That fact hurt me somewhere deep inside. It was like a thorn had embedded itself within my heart, constantly pricking away at me.

"Pff, ha, ha ha ha... Oh, how silly... That's what you're worried about?" Noname almost doubled over from laughter.

"Huh?" I said, flummoxed.

Unsure of how to take this, I looked to Suimei for help, but he was already giving me this fed-up look. "Real, not real... Who cares."

"The two of you are closer than most blood-related families are, and you still have that kind of worry? I'm sorry, but that's hilarious, dear."

"Oh, come on..." I mumbled. Did they think I was overthinking things?

Just as I started to feel huffy, Noname cooed, "You don't need to worry about a thing. In fact...if you really love that dullard, trust him."

*Trust him*—the meaning of those words eluded me, but I clung to them regardless.

She poked the gratin with her fork and giggled. "That man dotes on you like you're his world. Am I wrong?"

"No..." I admitted.

Unexpectedly, Suimei followed up Noname's words. "Why don't you ask him what he's doing yourself, the next time you meet? You said it yourself, right? You have to communicate, or your feelings won't be clear."

"Right... I did say that." For some reason, I felt like crying.

I buried my face into the table and, being ever-stubborn, grumbled, "I get it... I really do... But I can't stop thinking that I wouldn't be this worried if I were his daughter by blood..."

Noname sighed. "That is a matter of your own heart."

Slowly, I shut my eyelids.

What was essential was invisible to the eye. I understood that, I really did—but I still couldn't stop myself from searching among the things I could see. Even though it hurt so much.

The five of us had a peaceful dinner after that.

All the Shinonome-san stuff still weighed on me, but I decided to stop fretting about it as much as I could. That didn't mean I felt better about it all, but I certainly wasn't about to let myself agonize over it forever. For now, it could be pushed to the back of my mind.

We talked about many things, and before we knew it, it had grown late. I left the cleanup to Suimei and Kuro and got ready

THE HIDDEN HOUSE ON TONO MOUNTAIN

to go home. Noname walked me to the door. Just as I was about to leave, I decided to ask her one last time: "...You sure you don't know where Shinonome-san might be?"

"Nope. Not at all."

"And you won't tell me what he might be doing?"

She smiled. "He asked me to keep it a secret, so no."

I pursed my lips.

Nyaa-san, by my feet, frowned. "Won't budge, huh?"

Noname laughed her gorgeous laugh. "You best ask him yourself. It'll be more moving that way."

"Hm?"

"C'mon, tell us," Nyaa-san urged. "What's that blockhead playing at?"

"Sorry, but you won't be hearing anything from me. This apothecary's lips are tight. People would lose faith in my business if I went and blabbed secrets, after all."

I had to wonder, was it really such a big secret?

Nyaa-san and I shared a look.

That was when Noname's eyes suddenly lit up as she spotted something behind me. "My, what perfect timing! Now there's a man so loose-lipped you'd think it was his job." She smiled craftily. "You should ask *him*, dear. In fact, he's one of the ringleaders in all this mess. I don't want to hide anything from you anymore, my sweet Kaori, so go interrogate him, okay? Hey, Nyaa?"

"What?"

"Go catch that man!"

"All right...but I'm doing it for Kaori." Nyaa-san took off, gradually transforming into her giant form as she ran and tackled a passerby.

"Aaahhhhh?!"

"Nyaa-san?! What are you—wait, it's you?!" After a short trot, I found Nyaa-san using her foot to pin down a man dressed in an absurdly gaudy haori.

He struggled for a bit, but soon went limp and said, "I assure you that I would make for a terrible meal... But if you insist on giving me a taste regardless, I'll offer you something even better instead: one hundred hard-to-come-by stories. How about it?"

It was Shinonome-san's longtime friend, the shady-looking story-seller, Tamaki-san.

Having learned Shinonome-san's location from Tamaki-san, I returned to the shop to make some preparations and then quickly set off with Nyaa-san.

We went through the Hell of Great Wailing, the fifth of the Eight Hot Hells, to get where we needed. Surrounding the wailing dead was a steep stone wall. On that wall was a cave that connected to Iwate Prefecture, one of the six prefectures in Tohoku. More specifically, it connected to Mount Rokko-Ishi, located on the borders of Tono City and Kamaishi City.

We passed through the rugged cave and came out the other side. Because we had left after dinner, it was already dark out. Not a single cloud blotted the sky, allowing us to clearly see all the stars spread across it. Far off in the distance, I could faintly make out the peaks of the Kitagami Mountains as they were lit by starlight.

The nearby city of Tono was famous for its plentiful surviving folklore, so much so that it was known as "the Village of Folklore." Around here, non-humans and humans had existed in close proximity for ages. Perhaps thanks to that, many spirits still lived there today.

"It's cold." My warm breath formed a white cloud before fading away. It was too early for snow in Tohoku, but that didn't mean the nights weren't cold.

Nyaa-san wordlessly brushed up beside me. I happily accepted her kindness and clung to her body for warmth. Just then, a blue-white light appeared and slowly neared.

"You've come..." said an old lady in rags. She held a paper lantern with a blue Hitodama inside. Hitodama were these floating balls of fire thought to be human souls that had wandered away from their bodies. The old lady's hair was white and disheveled, clearly unbrushed. Her skin was dry, cracked like the surface of rock, and her cloudy eyes were clogged with yellow eye mucus. Finally, her arms and legs were as thin as twigs, and she walked barefoot. "Tamaki-sama asked me to guide you. Follow me."

She turned away and walked, her footsteps so quiet that she could've been sliding across ice. Nyaa-san and I shared a look and nodded before following after her. Only the light of the paper lantern helped us navigate the overgrown undergrowth of the dark mountain.

"We've had many guests as of late. How very unusual." The woman cackled before swiftly making her way down an animal trail. It took no small effort to keep up with her.

"Are you an acquaintance of Tamaki-san?" I asked.

She stopped and spun around, flashing a broad smile. "I am indebted to that man. He looks after me...a spirit who's but a shadow of the human she once was." She resumed walking. "Those who've fallen to the waysides of society have nowhere to go, you see."

Her words came as a bit of a surprise.

There were roughly three kinds of spirits. The first kind were those who were simply born as spirits. The second kind were objects that had gained sentience over many years. The third kind were former *humans* who had somehow become spirits.

Yao Bikuni was of the third kind. There weren't many former-human spirits around, but this old lady was apparently one of them.

With a sad smile on her face, she touched a nearby tree as she walked by it. In an instant, the air began to shift around us. Nyaa-san and I both stopped, wary of our surroundings.

The old lady laughed, giving us a gap-toothed smile. "It's nothing, we just passed through a boundary. C'mon now, let's continue."

"R-right," I stammered back.

"Kaori. Get on my back," Nyaa-san offered, not letting her guard down one bit.

"Good idea." I hopped onto Nyaa-san's back. She then continued to follow after the old lady.

The old lady touched a few more trees as we walked, causing the air to shift again and again. According to her, the mountain was split into various different areas, each ruled by its own land or mountain gods. The air felt different depending on the ruler of the specific area into which we had passed.

"We're here," she said.

After a long walk, we reached a wide, gaping clearing in the forest. A single tree stood within it. If I looked carefully, I could detect signs of pruning that had been done to the tree. Perhaps humans had lived here at one point in the past.

"Take your shoes off under that pear tree there, then touch it and wish to be moved," she said.

"Okay... Thank you for showing us the way." I followed the woman's instructions, neatly placing my shoes under the tree and reaching out for the trunk—but I stopped short. "Um, before I go, can I have your name? I'd like to show you my gratitude sometime."

The woman blinked a few times in surprise, then wrinkled her face into a smile. "What a polite child you are. I don't need any gratitude, but I'll give you my name. A long time ago, I was born as Sada, daughter of Mosuke. Later, I became known as Noboto-no-Baba and have been called many things since...but I suppose I'm best known as Samuto-no-Baba. Really, I'm just another of the many who got spirited away as a wee child and became something non-human. Nobody special at all."

I thanked Samuto-no-Baba again and gave her my name in turn. She gave me another wrinkly grin and sat down on a nearby stump. "Well, I'll be waiting here for you two."

"We'll try to be quick," I said.

"No, no, enjoy yourself. I usually exist as a statue, so I hardly feel the time pass. Take your time...Kaori."

"Okay, I will. Again, thank you!" I waved goodbye, then touched the tree trunk. In an instant, the air around me shifted again. I looked ahead of me and saw something colorful beyond the pear tree. "...Whoa!"

There was a traditional L-shaped farmhouse with a thatched roof, common in the Tono area. That alone wasn't all that exceptional, but it had appeared out of thin air. Around the farmhouse were a bunch of deciduous trees that brightened the area with brilliant reds and yellows. My ears also picked up the sound of horse whinnies, cow moos, and chicken clucks coming from somewhere. The farmhouse was built the old-fashioned way, but its materials were all brand new. A bright light seeped out from within it, giving me the impression that it was warm inside. However, the inside was dead silent, and there was nothing to indicate anyone was waiting within.

I gulped and approached the farmhouse with Nyaa-san. It was no exaggeration to say that this place was the most famous legend in all Tono folklore: Mayoiga, a phantom house said to bring riches to all who visited. This was where I would find my adoptive father, Shinonome-san.

"Pardon the intrusion."

The inside of the farmhouse was peculiar to say the least. Just past the entrance was a dirt floor, and there was a horse stable right to the side. Raising livestock was common in Iwate, and in fact, in the past it had been famous for rearing robust horses. Perhaps that was why keeping the animals at home was normal there.

With the building's layout, the smoke from the stove would rise and flow toward the stable, heating it and the hay stored in the attic. This kept the horse warm during the periods of heavy winter snowfall that this area received. The horse was treated like family, as was detailed in many old tales—but that's for another time.

A step up from the dirt floor was a tatami-matted area. There, a lit hearth in the floor heated a suspended steaming iron pot. It looked as though somebody had been there moments ago. I gingerly slid open the sliding door dividing the large room I had entered but didn't find Shinonome-san.

"He's probably over here, Kaori." Nyaa-san sniffed the air and walked toward the back of the farmhouse. There, we found a sliding door more luxurious than the others. Maybe this was where the master of the house slept?

A warm light seeped through the elaborate transoms above the sliding doors. I could sense someone inside.

"All right... Let's go." After sharing a look with Nyaa-san, I opened the door.

There, a familiar back awaited me.

His only good short-sleeve kosode looked even more worn-out than usual. From underneath his collar, the camel-colored shirt he always wore peeked out. His hair was graying, and a light scale pattern covered his skin.

He scratched his neck with a fountain pen, a habit of his that I had long since grown accustomed to seeing. Surrounding the desk he faced were discarded drafts, crumpled balls of paper, and a tower of reference books.

"Shinonome-san?" I called. I received no response. I moved to where I could see his face and was about to try and get his attention again when...I stopped.

"Kaori? What's wrong?" Nyaa-san asked, a puzzled look on her face.

I backed away from him and left the room. "I don't think I should bother him when he's like this."

"Why not? You have every right to chew him out. Don't you remember how much grief he gave you?"

"It's fine. I want to let him focus." I headed for the kitchen. Atop the counter were vegetables still fresh with dew, as well as fresh meat and rice, all just begging to be used. This was just the magic of Mayoiga, I supposed. I didn't see anyone else here, but we were definitely being given a grand welcome.

"Maybe he would be happy if I made something...?" I grinned wryly at myself and opened the lid of a pot. It was filled to the brim with cold well water. "All right! Nyaa-san, mind helping out?"

"What're you doing?" she asked.

I smiled and, with a bit of pride, said, "My duty...as Shinonome-san's daughter!"

"Whew... I'm finally done!" Shinonome-san stretched up his arms and let himself flop back onto the tatami. On the desk was a neatly bundled manuscript, the pages slightly crumpled. Red and black ink was splotched here and there on the manuscript, making it almost as shabby as his short-sleeve kosode.

Having been waiting for him to finish, I said, "Well done. Do you want to eat or take a bath first?"

"Whoa?!" He shot up and crawled toward me on all fours. He then grabbed my cheeks with both hands and stared at me. "Huh? What? Am I so exhausted that I'm seeing things...?"

"You wouldn't exactly be able to touch me if you were."

"That's true." He squished my face for a bit, then smiled broadly to reveal white teeth. "...Yeah, that's my daughter, all right."

Embarrassed, I quickly waved his hands away. "Stop it. Which is it then, are you eating or bathing first?"

"Oh! Only my daughter could make such a grumpy face!"

"Enough!"

"Aha ha! Sorry, sorry. I'll eat first."

"Unbelievable, the nerve of this man..." I grumbled as I led him to the sunken hearth. Above the hearth was an iron pot suspended on a pot hook. White steam rose from the pot, which contained a stew.

Shinonome's face lit up the moment he saw what was in the pot. "Oh! Hittsumi!"

"I thought hittsumi would be nice, since we're in Iwate. I get the feeling you haven't had a decent meal in a while either, so I tried making it a bit lighter on the oils."

Hittsumi was a soup with roots from Iwate. It consisted of bits of wheat flour kneaded until it was as soft as earlobes and thrown into a pot together with root vegetables. The wheat flour was plucked and torn apart, a process called "hittsumu" in the local Iwate dialect, from which the dish derived its name. The exact ingredients and methods used varied from family to family, making it a dish that often reminded one of home.

"I'll bet you've been eating nothing but meat, so I made sure to put tons of veggies in," I said. "There's roots, mushrooms, and even scallion! I also added some chicken in there, but it's mainly vegetables."

"Can I drink...?"

"No way! You're in no condition to be drinking with your exhaustion."

"Guh..." he groaned.

I ignored him and grabbed the ladle.

My hittsumi had a shoyu base—specifically one that employed bonito, mirin, and dark soy sauce. There was chicken in it, as well as a healthy amount of root vegetables and mushrooms. The ingredients gave the soup more than ample savoriness, as well as a wonderfully balanced flavor that eased the body.

"Eat up." I scooped out a big helping of vegetables, then ladled the broth over them. The chicken fats swirled in the soy sauce-colored broth, dimly glistening under the light. The relaxing smell of soy sauce filled the surrounding space, stimulating my hunger. All of a sudden, I had the urge to eat a second dinner.

The sputtering of the pot served as pleasant background noise for the meal. I handed Shinonome-san the bowl, and he looked in it and smiled, his eyes softening.

"Where's Nyaa-san?" he asked.

"She got bored of waiting, so she went to see the horses."

"Oh."

We made meaningless small talk as I served out my own portion. I had already eaten, so I figured I'd keep my portion small, but—

"Dang, that's good!"

"Whoa!" Surprised by Shinonome-san's sudden outburst, I dropped the ladle into the ashes of the hearth. I quickly picked it up and glared at him. "Jeez! You haven't even said grace yet!"

"My bad. I couldn't wait any longer. It's been days since I've had some hot soup."

"What are you, a child?"

He took another sip of the soup and exclaimed, "Mmm, but this really is some good stuff. I think your food might be the best in the world." He burned his lips and blew on the soup, then began chewing away at the wheat flour bits that had turned brown from the broth.

I gazed down at my own bowl and slowly brought it to my lips. The soy sauce brought the complex mix of savory flavors together, and the wheat flour bits gave the soup a delicious consistency.

It was good, I will admit... But it didn't taste like anything amazing, as my tongue was long used to the flavor from all the taste testing. Still—

"Give me seconds! With lots of those wheat flour bits...and chicken too, if you would."

"Yes, yes..."

Shinonome-san wolfed down my food. He hardly ate when I wasn't around but always seemed to have an appetite when I was.

I took his bowl and hung my head to hide my smile. At the same time, I felt a sniffle coming on. My vision suddenly blurred with tears, and I quickly tried to pull myself together.

"This really is good," he said. "You should make this again sometime."

"Sure."

Our first meal together in a while was a warm one.

"Ah, so Tamaki told you where I was." Shinonome-san scratched his head, taking a puff from his pipe and putting on an awkward smile.

"I was surprised to hear you were in Mayoiga. Were you hoping to take something home and become a millionaire?" I asked.

"Of course not. I'm just borrowing the house; I wasn't invited here. Nothing'll happen even if I do bring something back."

"Is that right." I noticed Nyaa-san had been gone for a while now and wondered for a moment if she was all right. I then looked over at Shinonome-san and, with some anxiety, asked, "So, do you mind telling me what you're doing out here? It feels weird staying home all day, not knowing what you're up to."

*If Shinonome-san thinks of me as his real daughter...then he will tell me,* I thought.

He looked conflicted for a moment, then stood up and left for the room he had been in earlier. He came back bringing the bundled manuscript with which he had been locked in battle.

THE HIDDEN HOUSE ON TONO MOUNTAIN

"Take a look," he said.

"You sure?"

"Yeah. But not a word of its contents to anyone else."

Gingerly, I flipped through the pages. The instant I understood what they contained, my eyes shot up to meet his.

The pages held the names of spirits I knew, as well as spirits I didn't. It told of where they lived and their histories, and detailed what legends and folktales they were named in. Many of the stories he had received in lieu of money were also included.

Bashfully, he explained, "I—no, a group of us are planning to publish a spirit realm anthology."

"A what?"

"An anthology, a collection of stories. It'll contain tales about the spirit realm and offer information on spirits and their legends. Not bad, right?"

I looked down at the manuscript again. Forget not bad, it was incredible. The human world had various encyclopedias and other resources detailing the tales and origins of spirits, but never has there been any *direct* accounts compiled by spirits themselves. By reading this, you could learn the true lives spirits lived. Merely academically speaking, this was an invaluable resource. It would definitely make an amazing book!

"This is incredible, Shinonome-san! Wait, has a book ever been published in the spirit realm before?"

"Nope, it'll be a first for us. An acquaintance of mine has some connections to a printing company that we're hoping to use. If things go through, we'll be blazing new trails," he said proudly.

With the advent of media and the development of capitalist commerce, spirits had gradually become thought of as imaginary, fictional things. The humans of old had once believed in the existence of spirits and regarded them with fear and wariness. But as the eras passed, a rift formed between humans and spirits. Now, most humans have never seen a spirit before, in part due to more and more spirits moving to the spirit realm.

As a result, books that detailed new, firsthand accounts of spirits had disappeared entirely. Writing stories was a human activity, and spirits existed through being remembered, so only the most famous of spirits were recorded while the others gradually faded away in name and form.

"That's why we're trying to make our lives remembered, to try and decrease the number of spirits that become forgotten, if even just by one," he said.

I remembered something as I listened to his explanation. Our bookstore kept track of our most popular books, and many of them were books by Toriyama Sekien, an ukiyo-e illustrator from the 1700s who often drew spirits. Our Toriyama Sekien books were almost always out on loan to someone. They had very few words in them, being illustrated books, so I always wondered why they were so popular...but now I think I understood. The spirits who borrowed those books saw their own lives portrayed—and remembered—in his work.

Shinonome-san looked a bit somber as he took a drag from his pipe. Exhaling smoke, he said, "For the longest time, I thought there was nothing that could be done about spirits who went unrecorded and were forgotten. But Tamaki said we could change that—that we could make the impossible possible. 'The only thing holding us back is our belief it's impossible,' kinda stuff."

"You're talking about how spirits can't write books and stories?"

He nodded, staring at his ink-stained hands. "That's when I remembered: when you were young, I kept a journal to record your growth. So, I took it out and read it. Turns out it was a surprisingly good read. Nothing compared to actual commercial books, of course, but it was readable. Without even realizing it, I had created something."

Furthermore, while doing his work at the bookstore, he learned his patrons had interesting experiences of their own to tell. They would regale friends and families with these experiences, adding little embellishments here and there to make the stories more interesting. Sometimes, the stories would even be retold in different ways by other people. While their originators might not have intended it, in so doing, they made something *original*. Such a chain of exchanges was no different from the sort of practice that humans had performed in the distant past.

"Spirits actually aren't all that different from humans," Shinonome-san said. "We've just never *thought* to write books ourselves..."

With that realization, he began collecting and writing down stories from spirits who couldn't pay the store with money. He then sold those stories to Tamaki-san for the purpose of eventually compiling everything into a book.

"Nuh-uh—I remember you taking stories in place of money way back when I was a child!"

"Heh heh. That's because I've been working on this for over ten years now! Incredible, right?" Shinonome-san said proudly, putting a hand over the manuscript. "A long time ago, books used to be real expensive, so a bunch of literary scholars opened up a book-lending store to let more people read. The book-lender was so popular during the war period that people were borrowing books left and right whenever an air raid wasn't happening. Eventually, the books they had on hand weren't enough, so they started self-publishing. It's weird. Before I knew it, I was doing the same thing. Humans and spirits have their differences, but we take similar paths in life."

He got more worked up and exclaimed, "This book covers just about every spirit there is in the spirit realm! There's no way it won't be a hit! If Tamaki were here, he'd say it perfectly targets demand or whatever! Word of mouth will spread once people realize their own stories are in here, and then tons and tons of spirits will come and borrow this book, don't you think?"

"I guess?"

"Well, once that happens, we can live easy. You won't need to pick up part-time work anymore."

"Huh?" I was left speechless.

Shinonome-san reached out his large hand and roughly made a mess of my hair. "I can't stay a deadbeat dad forever, now can I? I'm going to publish this book and become a father who can provide enough for his daughter to eat; a father you can be proud of... Will you help me?"

This was Shinonome-san's grand dream: publishing the first ever book in the spirit realm. It wasn't just an attempt to emulate what had until now been solely a human activity, nor merely an attempt to leave his mark on the world. It was for me... Shinonome-san was breaking new ground for me, his daughter!

He looked a little more haggard than usual, but his blue-gray eyes shone like a hopeful young boy's.

*Oh, Shinonome-san...* I nodded deeply, my chest warm. The memory of that promise I'd made with him long ago surfaced to mind, the one sworn underneath that starry sky. He had found it. Even as an adult, he'd found the *something* he wanted to be.

"I'll help you. Of course I'll help you!" I said.

"I'm not being a bother?"

"Of course not. I'd be more than glad to help you...Father." I smiled.

My father's stiff face softened as he pulled me into a tight hug. Rubbing his unshaved chin against my cheeks, he exclaimed, "Oh, Kaori... I swear, I'll make this book a success!"

"Ow, your stubble! Ow, ow!"

From the bottom of my heart, I was glad I had taken the plunge and asked him what he was up to.

I reaffirmed to myself what I wanted to do from here: I wanted to help him. I wanted to treasure what we had. I wanted to be the best daughter I could be for him, even if we weren't bound by blood. To that end, I could endure a bit of stubble.

I grinned wryly as I closed my eyes and endured the prickling.

Suddenly, I heard what sounded like paper tearing close by. Worried we had accidentally torn his manuscript, I quickly looked down. But the precious manuscript was fine.

"Shinonome-san, did you hear..." My voice trailed off as his strong arms slackened, and I felt his comforting warmth slip away from me. "...Shinonome-san?"

With a thud, he slammed onto the tatami mat. His skin was covered in fissures, like cracks on pottery...or paper torn, then smushed together.

"K-Kao... Kaori..." Slowly, he extended a hand toward me.

Confused as to what was happening, I extended a hand to him as well. But when my fingers met his, I heard the sound of paper tearing again. It was an unsettling sound, one that shook my eardrums.

Scared, I tried to hug him. He looked me in the eyes, his face pale, and tried to reassure me. "I-I'm...okay... Don't...worry."

Without warning, his body vanished into thin air, as though it had never been real. The adoptive father who had protected me, raised me—he was gone, leaving not a trace of his warmth behind.

"No..." I clutched my arms and crouched. For some reason, it was suddenly so, so unbearably cold. I needed the warmth of another. I needed the warmth of that big, strong, reliable father who protected me. "No!"

My mind went blank as I wailed like a child.

# CHAPTER 4

# The Wakasa Meditation Cave

"THERE, THERE, don't cry."

Whenever I cried when I was little, Shinonome-san would soothe me with those words. He would pat my back as he held my small body in his arms, and he was always gentle with me, despite normally acting so rough. I always calmed down in his arms, slowly dozing off into sleep as I became fatigued from all the crying. He would begin to gently rock me then, something he had been taught to do by Noname and the young wife next door, but he was always a little awkward with it.

*One-two-three, one-two, one-two...*

The broken rhythm of his rocking would at times stir me awake. But I never minded. I simply hugged my short arms around his neck and shut my eyes again.

"Everything's going to be all right, Kaori. I'm right here."

I remember he once admitted that he was too embarrassed to sing me lullabies, which was why he comforted me with words instead.

The smell of sweat and tobacco that clung to him, and the tender words with which he soothed me—everything about him made me feel safe, like I was wrapped tight by his very essence.

After Shinonome-san disappeared, Nyaa-san and I hurried back to the spirit realm. I wanted to believe his disappearance wasn't real, that maybe he was already home at the bookstore, waiting for me.

It was already late at night. The town was completely silent and still as death, dimly lit only by the reddish sky. The main street, now vacant, felt foreign to me. There were no shopkeepers to call out to me, no neighbors to stop and chat with. This town had no warmth to show me, only this cold air that mercilessly coiled around my body.

When we did reach the bookstore, we immediately searched every nook and cranny of the shop and the living space. But the cold, lightless home yielded no sign of my father.

Wanting to cry, I squatted down on the roadside, but for some reason, the tears wouldn't come. The worrisome thoughts clouding my mind and the unease swirling in my chest needed an outlet to vent through, but the tears just wouldn't flow. Instead, I felt a profound emptiness inside me.

Had I run dry of emotion…? No. I could feel the maelstrom of emotions inside me still; I just couldn't express them. Sadness. Fear. Regret. I couldn't tell them apart from one another now.

I couldn't help but smile wryly at the realization. I was just like how a certain former exorcist had been up until a little while ago.

"I guess I'm not one to talk now, am I...?" I muttered. I hugged my knees and shut my eyes.

Nyaa-san returned from searching the perimeter of the store. "Nothing... Shoot, just where could that idiot be?!" She whacked her three tails against the ground in frustration and told me to get on her back.

"Where are we going?" I asked.

"Where do you think?" she said before taking off for the apothecary, where Noname, the one who had raised me in place of a mother, would be.

Being late, the apothecary was closed. But there was still some faint light coming from the back, indicating someone was awake. I wondered whether I should wrap around to the back entrance when a voice called out to me.

"Kaori?" It was Suimei, surrounded by glimmerflies and together with Kuro.

Nyaa-san walked over to Kuro. "Hey, mutt. We need to talk."

"Huh? T-talk? With me?"

She gave him a quick, meaningful glance before walking away. Reluctantly, he followed.

"Huh? Nyaa-san? Wait..." I said.

"I'll be right back. Suimei, look after Kaori for me." She and Kuro slipped away into the darkness.

The moment she left my sight, I became overwhelmed with

unease. She always liked to take action by herself, so why did I feel so awful? I felt like I had returned to being a helpless child.

I took a deep sigh and pulled myself together, then faced Suimei. "Were you out somewhere?"

He shook his head. "Just cooling my head."

"Your head? Were you angry or something?"

"It's nothing. All in the past."

"Well, all right. I have some business with Noname. Can I come in?"

He nodded, taking a key out of his pocket and opening the door. He then stopped, turned around, and slowly held his hand out to me.

"Huh?" I was at a loss as to how I was supposed to respond to the strange gesture.

He muttered, "I can tell something's wrong from the look on your face. Take my hand."

I stared back at him in shock.

"I don't know what happened, but you can at least let me help," he said. Seeing me still not move, he half-forcibly grabbed my hand and led me through the door.

His palm was warm. The chill of the night slowly faded from my body, starting with my fingers.

*Ah, I'm so glad he isn't looking right now... If he saw my face, he'd get all worried again...*

I matched his pace with my gaze down; that way, on the off

chance he turned around, he wouldn't see the tears streaming down my face.

We passed through the store and entered the courtyard, which smelled of tea olives. I found Noname with a grim look on her face and Tamaki-san as his usual peculiar self.

"Well, if it isn't the bookstore girl," Tamaki-san greeted us. "Did you manage to meet Shinonome? You look rather pale, though; did something bad happen? That makes two of us I suppose. Look at me, don't I look like one of those storied warriors knocking on death's door?"

He grimaced and lightly touched his body. He was covered in scars all over. I thought for a moment that it might be because Nyaa-san was holding him down with her foot, but on further thought, that alone couldn't explain the severity of his injuries.

"You reap what you sow. Just how much trouble do you think you caused Suimei and Kuro?" Noname spat, glaring at him with the incensed visage of a demon. "You're always like this, stirring up trouble and leaving once you've had your fill. Take some responsibility for your actions for once. Awful, just awful. When I heard what you did from Suimei, I thought I'd actually kill you."

"Ha ha, you got me pegged there. But here's the thing, Miss: If it weren't for me stirring up trouble in the first place, that exorcist boy wouldn't be here. It was all part of a carefully laid plan of mine, so being able to enjoy the story that followed it is my right, is it not?"

"Oh, you be quiet!" Noname's face was red with anger. It wasn't often that she lost her cool like this, usually being the one to crack jokes instead. In contrast to her, Tamaki-san wore an aloof smile.

Suimei, on the other hand, looked a little glum. It felt as though he were tackling some complicated emotions. Worried, I asked, "Are you all right?"

"I'm fine. If it weren't for that man, I'd be worse off right now. I owe him, even if he didn't do anything directly to help me. But..." He hesitated for a moment, then looked directly at Tamaki-san. "I don't trust him. He's not an enemy, but he's no ally either."

"Humph, is that so, young man?" Tamaki-san said. "I suppose that's one way to read things."

"Well said, Suimei," Noname said. "You absolutely mustn't trust this fool. Oh, I know. Let's tell Shinonome what he did. See how you like that!"

"Please, anything but that!" Tamaki-san groaned. "That man is uncontrollable when he loses it. I enjoy conflict as a narrative device, but not when it involves me!"

It had slipped my mind until now, but the only times Tamaki-san actually had the upper hand on Shinonome-san was when he was collecting my father's manuscripts. Generally, Shinonome-san was the one hounding Tamaki-san for something or another. I've seen Shinonome-san chew Tamaki-san out over drinks so many times, it didn't even come as a surprise anymore.

"I don't know what you did," I said, "but try not to give Shinonome-san too much to worry about. He has enough on his plate already..." My chest tightened as I suddenly remembered why I'd come. I broke into a cold sweat, feeling guilty for having forgotten at all.

"Kaori?" Noname asked, looking at me worriedly.

Distressed, I hugged her. Her flowery scent enveloped me as I buried my face into her firm chest. She hugged me back and whispered, "What's wrong? Did something happen? I'm sorry, I was so preoccupied with Tamaki that I didn't notice. What could have brought you here this late?"

I steadied my breathing and looked up. "I-I don't know what to do. Help me. Shinonome-san has disappeared!"

I explained everything that had happened: from my visit to Mayoiga to our meal together, from the moment I learned his dream—to the moment he suddenly vanished.

The first to speak was Tamaki-san, sounding surprised. "He told you, huh? And after all that hollering about keeping it a secret to surprise you. That man's got no backbone. No fore-shadowing this way either."

"You be quiet," Noname snapped. "Kaori, you said he vanished?"

"Yeah. There was a sound similar to paper tearing...and then he disappeared, like he was never there in the first place." I shud-dered. The possibility that our entire life together had been an illusion crossed my mind and made me feel unsteady. My legs gave away as I sank to the floor.

Noname helped me back up. I looked up to thank her but stopped when I saw a face scarier than any other I had seen before. "Tamaki, do you know anything about this?" she asked.

Tamaki-san shrugged, just a bit. "I might."

In an instant, the hand that had been helping me up disappeared. I fell flat on my behind while Noname suddenly appeared next to Tamaki-san. She lunged a hand at his face and dug her long, painted green nails into his cheeks.

"Bastard... Spit out what you know, right this instant." My hair stood on end as Noname's speech lost all its usual femininity, forgotten in her anger.

Tamaki-san sweated profusely and slapped against her arm, expressing surrender.

"Noname, he can't talk like that," Suimei pointed out.

"Oh my, I'm so sorry. I don't know what came over me," she said, releasing Tamaki-san's face.

Now freed, Tamaki-san looked up at her wearily. "Ha ha. You always get so worked up whenever Shinonome is involved. How very inter—*h-hey*, hey, hey, I'm joking, I'm joking. Cut me some slack already. I'm but a humble story-seller, born with a silver book in my arms—I'm not a fighter!"

He quickly straightened himself in his seat and cleared his throat. Then he began telling us what he knew. "Whenever something new is created, there will be some resistance. That is especially true here in the spirit realm. I suspect those opposed to change have taken action."

The spirit realm could be defined by two things: stagnation and slow change. Unlike the human world, where change occurred at dizzying speeds, the spirit realm was where the old came to linger. By human world standards, spirits were ancient. So, by extension, it could have been said that the spirit realm was a place where archaic, unchanging things gathered.

"This is how I interpret it," Tamaki-san continued. "The spirit realm contains many people who value things staying the same. People who are very afraid of change."

Shinonome-san's attempt at publishing a book was a monumental first for the spirit realm. A spirit was *creating* something. No longer would everything have to come from the human world. Furthermore, if he succeeded, he wouldn't be the last. Creations upon creations would surely spring up in his wake.

Tamaki-san went on. "If Shinonome publishes his book, the spirit realm won't sit quiet anymore. Creation breeds discussion, stimulates thoughts, moves emotions, stirs hearts. He will inspire leagues of spirits, and not just with his writing. His action will open the spirits' eyes to the realization that they too can create, and that is by no means a small thing. The urge to create is powerful, more so than you could possibly imagine. It might even shake the very foundations of the spirit realm..."

He narrowed his eyes, spellbound. His cheeks flushed, and his mouth hung half open. He then grandiosely extended his left arm, as though gesturing to the sky, and exclaimed, "We'll be rid of the ancient ways! The birth of the new is the death of the old! Ah, change... Change is glorious! All the spirits who spent their waking moments disinterested in the world will join hands and create! The old tomes will be thrown off the bookshelves and replaced with the new! Is it not sublime?"

He continued to ramble—*Old is bad! Old things spoil.*

*We must create new things!*—and such. I shared a look with Noname and Suimei, then smiled uneasily.

What he was saying sounded right. Stagnation could lead to things slipping through the cracks, like, for example, minor spirits who were never recorded in books and would eventually disappear. Those spirits needed change if they were to stay in this world; Shinonome-san had said such himself. But something about Tamaki-san's words was harder to accept than Shinonome-san's...

"We need to rid ourselves of the ancient ways. History? Tradition? All meaningless. The old will kneel before this revolutionary change," he declared.

It didn't sound so much like he wanted the new, but rather like he held a deep-seated loathing for the old. I couldn't so easily agree when I myself respected the value of both the old and the new.

After thinking for a bit, Noname heaved a great sigh. She ran a hand through her moss-green hair and coolly said, "Okay, I understand what you're saying...though there were a few things I disagreed with. But, supposedly, there are people out there willing to harm someone just because they're doing something new? I find that hard to believe."

"Really? If you look at human world history, it's not that far-fetched," he replied.

"Perhaps," she mused. "Let's leave the debates for later. Who's the one who kidnapped Shinonome? You have an idea, don't you?"

Tamaki-san stroked his neat chin hair thoughtfully. "I have someone in mind, yes."

"Y-you do?!" I exclaimed.

He smiled bitterly. "Are you that worried about your father? Well, it shouldn't take long at all for you to reach the culprit's location, but...there's a place I want you to go to first."

"Is doing so more important than saving Shinonome-san?" I asked.

"That it is." He narrowed his eyes, his clouded right eye peering straight at me. "It's the location of Shinonome's main body, after all."

We got to work moving the many mobile bookshelves in the bookstore in a specific order. The shelves were so heavy with books that they wouldn't even budge if I didn't put my back into pushing them.

In no time at all, the stairs leading to the basement appeared. A cold breeze of air came from below that made my skin pimple with gooseflesh, so I pulled on the cardigan I had kept on my shoulder.

"Shall we?" I swallowed and nodded at Noname.

"Let's." She nodded back, and together we proceeded down the stairs.

Shortly behind us, Tamaki-san, Nyaa-san, Suimei, and Kuro followed.

"So scary... Why's it so dark and cold?!"

"Be quiet, mutt. If it's such a problem, why don't you just head back? To the human world, that is."

"So mean! Why are you trying to chase me out of the spirit realm?!"

I listened to Nyaa-san and Kuro bicker as I wordlessly continued forward. The candle stand in the back was unlit, leaving the basement pitch-black, but I had expected as much and brought a paper lantern with some glimmerflies in it. The books that I could just barely make out looked untouched since the last time I'd seen them. The only thing different was that a single new spider web had been spun.

Cautiously, I stepped farther and farther into the back.

It was dark. The light of my paper lantern didn't reach all the way back, making me apprehensive that something might be lurking in the shadows. I should have been used to darkness, having been raised in a world of perpetual night, but knowing Shinonome-san's main body was back there shook me to the core.

Main body... Just what did that mean? Ordinary spirits didn't have such a thing. Shinonome-san had more than one secret he kept from me, and I didn't know how to feel about that.

"Huh?!"

But all my fears and worries were forgotten the moment I reached the back of the basement, where a shock awaited me. I shone a light over the red door, the sealed mystery that had held my wonder all these long years, to find its seals undone.

The seals should have been powerful! Suimei, a former exorcist, had said so himself!

"Well, would you look at that?" Tamaki-san said, amused. I couldn't even work up the urge to get angry at him.

I bent over and picked up one of the talismans fallen on the floor. I couldn't feel any power from the spell scrawled on it in cinnabar ink. From behind me, I heard Suimei and Tamaki-san talking.

"This was no weak talisman," Suimei said. "We must be up against a powerful spirit if they could break it this easily."

"Oh, I wonder about that," Tamaki-san replied. "If you ask me, this talisman looks like it'd be fairly ineffective against non-spirits."

"You're saying the culprit's a human? Are there any humans other than Kaori and me in the spirit realm?"

"Now, how should I answer that? Hmm, how about you think for yourself? It wouldn't be much of a story if the detective gave away the answer so easily, now would it?"

"This isn't some mystery novel; you're just being a jerk."

"Like I always say, you're free to interpret things how you like. I've been kind enough, but whether you receive that kindness is up to you." Tamaki-san smiled. It irked me how he always withheld information when he clearly knew so much more.

I left the two to their own devices and picked up the rest of the talismans, slowly making my way to the red door. I held the paper lantern up to find the door itself was broken. It appeared to have been smashed by something blunt and was covered in dents.

"I can smell Shinonome-san back there!" Kuro said after a sniff. Then he ran through the door.

I soon followed, entering a small, nearly empty room about three and a half square meters large. There were no windows, no shelves, and no furnishings. There was only a torn scroll hanging against the back wall.

"Huh? There's nothing here but a hanging scroll. Where's Shinonome?" Kuro asked, sniffing the air.

I neared the hanging scroll and stared at it. "It couldn't be..."

It was an ink wash painting depicting a dragon. The dragon was long and narrow, and it gracefully snaked between clouds. Unfortunately, the lower half was torn away, leaving its whole composition a mystery.

"Shinonome...san?" Gently, I touched the dragon on the hanging scroll. It looked so alive, it was hard to believe it had been drawn from ink. I could clearly make out the detail of each individual scale, all reflecting sunlight like the dragon was flying before me. Its long, coiling body was breathtaking; I could have stared at it all day. And its eyes. Its eyes seemed to peer into my soul, while also showing the depths of its own...

I stared, utterly captivated. As I did, *color* began to seep into the painting. Its monotone gray palette grew vivid before my eyes, taking on a blinding golden yellow. It was a color reminiscent of ripe, plentiful, wind-swept fields, as well as the evening glow of sunset—the color of autumn.

"It's beautiful," I said softly.

Suddenly, Noname covered my eyes. "No more looking, dear."

"Why?" I asked, moving away her hand.

After a moment's hesitation, she said, "...Humans become charmed if they look at it too long."

"Huh? What do you mean?"

"This scroll has a strange power within it." She shook her head sadly before somberly continuing. "It is a cursed scroll said to bring its owner good fortune."

"It brings good fortune, but it's cursed?" I asked.

"That's right. Many humans desired its effects, fighting and even killing for it. It breeds conflict, so it is cursed. And Shinonome is...the Tsukumogami of this scroll."

"Oh."

Shinonome-san was a Tsukumogami.

I hadn't realized it until now, but I knew very little about him. I didn't even know where he'd come from or how he'd come to run the bookstore. And I wanted to be his daughter? How could I be so despicable?

I balled my hand into a fist and sadly murmured, "I want to know more about Shinonome-san."

Noname smiled lovingly and hugged me. "You can ask him yourself. Don't worry, he's not dead yet."

"Really?! But the lower half of the scroll's gone... Is he really okay?!"

"Yes. If he were really dead, we wouldn't even have the remains in this room." She nodded deeply to reassure me.

I let out a sigh of relief. That was when Tamaki-san came in, holding something. He handed it to me with a grin that rubbed me wrong. "I'm proud to say I've never incorrectly predicted the culprit in a mystery novel. The one who abducted Shinonome is now confirmed to be a former human, like I thought. That's how they got through the seals so easily. They were pretty boastful about it too, as they left some flowers behind. Although, I'll bet our culprit isn't as pure of heart as those flowers."

I looked down at what he gave me—a bouquet of five spotless, pure-white flowers with yellow stamens. The deep green leaves contrasted beautifully with the white petals.

White camellia. They had been plucked, stem and all, at the height of their bloom.

It had been a long, long day. It felt like forever ago that I'd waited for Shinonome-san to return home so we could eat baked sweet potatoes, when really it had been only the day before.

The sky of the human world brightened as morning finally arrived. Birds flew off toward the sun as though to welcome it. The air was clear and had that penetrating chill that forced people awake.

We had wasted no time and immediately set out after finding the white camellias in the basement of the bookstore. Wordlessly, we passed through one of the hells and made for our destination. The trip reminded me of that one time we went to Okinawa. Kuro had been so frightened then. This time, however, he stayed nice and quiet in Suimei's arms.

Unexpectedly, Tamaki-san also came along without muttering a single complaint. He was as shady about it as ever, but he guided us to our destination without any trouble.

The place he guided us to was Kuinji Temple, a Buddhist temple in Obama City, Fukui Prefecture. In the second year of the Daiei era (year 1522 by the Gregorian calendar), Takeda Motomitsu, then governor of the Wakasa Province, relocated to Wakasa from Kyoto and built Nochiseyama Castle. He lived nearby, at the foot of the mountain the castle rested on. The ruins of his residence later became Kuinji Temple, which now held his family grave.

"Our culprit has close ties to this place," Tamaki-san said as he proceeded onto the temple grounds.

The small mountain nearby must have been Nochiseyama Mountain. It was still dawn, but I could faintly make out the colorful red and yellow leaves adorning it.

I followed Tamaki-san and sighed, my white breath soon fading into the air. I hadn't had a wink of sleep, but strangely, I wasn't tired at all. Perhaps my nerves, strung tight by my worry for Shinonome-san, forced me to remain awake.

"Please don't push yourself, Kaori," Noname murmured.

*If I don't push myself now, then when?* I thought with a bitter smile. Of course, I didn't say as much.

Noname's expression clouded. It stung my heart, but I couldn't back down here. I had to save Shinonome-san, at all costs.

After a short walk, Tamaki-san came to a stop. Before us was a well-kept hedge and a wooden fence. Beyond it was a large cave entrance on the surface of the mountain.

I jumped a bit the moment I saw the figure near the cave entrance. "...Oh. It's just a stone statue," I realized, calming down.

The stone statue was carved in the image of a person. The person, a Buddhist nun, held a flower in one hand, one that seemed to shine white in the morning sunlight. My chest grew tight as I recognized the depiction of the fair-skinned nun—Yao Bikuni.

This place was Yao Bikuni's Meditation Cave, the place she had chosen as her final resting place.

The cave was dark and narrow, and the ceiling was only about one-and-a-half meters high. There was just enough room for two people to walk shoulder to shoulder, and the back wasn't far away at all. The only thing inside was a lonely stone tablet.

This cave was where Yao Bikuni had entered her final meditation, also known as nyujo. Nyujo was a practice in Shingon Esoteric Buddhism where a monk entered eternal meditation to posthumously lead the masses to enlightenment. A practitioner would fast as they rang a bell and chanted sutras...until eventually, their body passed away and mummified.

But I knew Yao Bikuni was still active in the spirit realm, so it was a little hard for me to believe she had died and become a mummy here.

As soon as we set foot into the cave, Tamaki-san spun around and proudly said, "Now's the time for this story-seller to shine. Allow me to tell you the sad tale of a young woman, one that'll surely bring you to tears."

"What? We don't have time for that right now," I said.

"Ha ha. There's no need to rush, little miss. You know what they say: slow and steady wins the race. You're familiar with proverbs, no? I'd hope you are, being the daughter of a bookstore owner. How could you hope to understand books without knowing proverbs?"

I glared at him, but he simply laughed throatily. He put a hand to his chest and bowed slightly. "Besides, it is a story-seller's nature to want to tell stories. I understand you are so, sooo worried about your father... But I'm sure you can afford to lend an ear for a short while."

I continued to glare at him but didn't say anything. He seemed to take this as my answer and began telling his tale.

"Once upon a time, in a Wakasa village called Higashisei, there lived a young girl as beautiful as jade."

I listened reluctantly at first, but I was soon drawn in by his storytelling skill.

He told the story of how Yao Bikuni had come to be. When she was sixteen, her father was invited to another man's house for a dinner party. That man was not one of the many who had lived in the area for generations but a strange man who appeared suddenly one day, yet was somehow welcomed by all.

"That man had received an unknown, fragrant meat as a souvenir from the Palace of the Dragon King. He treated his guests to it, but the father refused to eat it, knowing it was mermaid meat."

The traditional Japanese image of mermaids differed slightly from their modern appearance. Mermaids had once been thought of as entirely fish from the shoulders down, with two pale arms and a child's head. The father had overheard the chefs discussing how to prepare such meat and even seen it firsthand before the meal.

"The father didn't eat the mermaid meat, but he did bring some home, thinking it'd make a nice story. Little did he know that it would change his daughter's life forever."

The daughter was curious about the meat her father brought back and ate a small cut. She then became enamored with its flavor and wound up eating the rest of the mermaid meat. From then on, she never aged a day.

"This is where our tragedy begins." Tamaki-san smiled creepily and extended his left arm with full grandeur. "The girl was terribly beautiful and so was wed into a wealthy family. The husband was kind and loved her from the bottom of his heart, and the girl became very happy. But don't forget: the girl didn't age. Her beloved *changed* with time, getting older; but she herself remained the *same*! Oh, how terrible. Don't you think so, little miss?"

As though he were telling a great joke, Tamaki-san tried his best to hold in laughter. I felt a bit disgusted; there was nothing funny about the story at all. Watching the one you loved grow old, then staying by their side as they died, had to feel terrible.

He continued, "The girl went on to marry many other people. But they all eventually died, leaving her behind. According to some accounts, she married around three hundred and nineteen people."

"That many...?"

"Yes. It's quite a lot, isn't it? And she had to watch them all on their deathbed. But that's not all. You see, humans dislike those different from them. Gradually, the villagers began to ostracize her."

So the girl ran away from her hometown. She then shaved off her precious hair and became a nun, beginning a pilgrimage around the country as Yao Bikuni.

"Folktales of Yao Bikuni exist all over Japan. Tales of her saving people and preaching the faith; tales of her planting cedar trees and camellias—all are still told to this day... Eventually, she returned here, her hometown. All so—"

"I could give this life its long-overdue death."

Suddenly, a pale arm reached out from the back of the cave. "Guh!"

"You sure can run your mouth. Are all story-sellers this annoying?"

The pale arm wrapped around Tamaki-san's neck and strangled him. The color quickly drained from his face.

"Let him go!" The first to react was Suimei. He quickly reached into his pouch and threw a talisman. It stuck to the pale arm and began to burn its skin.

"Humph." The arm released Tamaki-san, now unconscious, but grabbed his collar and dragged him deeper into the cave.

"Kuro!" Suimei called.

"On it!" Kuro took off like the wind. Tamaki-san suddenly disappeared into the back of the cave, and then so did Kuro.

"Kuro! Tamaki-san!" I yelled. But I received no response. Worried, I turned around, only for something to slip past me—Nyaa-san.

She observed her surroundings carefully, inspecting the space behind the stone tablet, when, without warning, the front half of her body *sunk* into the wall.

"Wha—Nyaa-san?!" I screamed.

"Kaori, please quiet down a bit," she said, turning around like nothing had happened. She looked at the back wall again and flicked her three tails. "It looks like we can continue farther. I don't really know how, but there's a really wide space ahead."

"How strange," Noname muttered, furrowing her brows.

"We shouldn't be able to continue past this point. There used to be a space back there, but that was a long time ago. Come to think of it, I heard the high priest of Kuinji Temple once went back there for his own amusement and came out in the middle of Tanba Mountain. Is the space warped? No, that couldn't be. This isn't the spirit realm. Just where is this connected to?"

She sighed, then said to me, "But then again, what choice do we have but to go?"

"Right." I nodded and gritted my teeth as I looked at the back of the cave.

Honestly, I was scared. I had no idea what was waiting for me on the other side of the wall. But I had to go, to save Shinonome-san. As his daughter, I had to go!

Someone came up beside me and grabbed my hand. Surprised, I turned and saw Suimei, expressionless like always.

"Don't worry. I'll protect you," he said.

"What...?"

"Don't try to do everything yourself. We're here with you. Didn't I tell you that you could let me help?"

I looked around me. My best friend, Nyaa-san, was here. The one who'd raised me like a mother, Noname, was here... And Suimei was here. The three of them were strong, unlike regular old me. They were people I could count on.

Of course. How could I have forgotten? I was with people I could depend on. The moment I realized that, my shoulders relaxed and the fog in my mind cleared. I then noticed Suimei looked a little pale.

*Right. Kuro is Suimei's dear partner. He must be racked with worry right now, but he stayed behind to comfort me.*

"I'm sorry I made you worry," I said. "I hope Kuro's all right. Let's go."

"Let's."

I clenched his hand tightly and stepped forward, deeper into the cave. Behind me, I heard Noname and Nyaa-san saying something.

"Oh, to be young! How wonderful! That's youth for you, dear. If only I were a thousand years younger..."

"You think the two of them have something going on, Noname?"

"Absolutely! Though they haven't realized it themselves, it seems!" Noname said in high spirits before calmly continuing. "We better hurry up and report this to that dunce, Shinonome, or he'll whine something about his daughter being stolen from under his nose. Honestly, that man can be such a handful."

"Good grief... Why's that old man never around when it matters?"

"Right?!"

The two heaved a great sigh together.

I turned around and urged them forward. "C'mon, let's go!"

The two nonchalantly followed after me as though they had all the time in the world.

"'When the white camellias wither, know that I am no longer of this world'... That was what I told everyone before I entered this cave many years ago. Yet, even this year, those pure-white, unsullied flowers bloom again."

Suimei and I held hands as we stepped past the back wall. Like Nyaa-san had said, the space continued further within. There was a split in the ceiling that allowed a single ray of morning sun to shine through, but the surroundings were still overwhelmingly dark and only faintly visible. Strange stone objects lined the walls, occasionally giving me a fright as I mistook their shapes for people.

Yao Bikuni was waiting for us, wearing the same smile she had showed us in the spirit realm. She brought a white camellia to her nose and frowned slightly, before artlessly tossing it to the ground. "Camellias have such a weak scent... Welcome. It's not much to look at, but please, enjoy your stay in my humble abode."

"Where's Shinonome-san?! And Kuro and Tamaki-san!" I demanded.

Yao Bikuni casually lifted an arm and pointed toward a line of strangely shaped stone objects.

"Shinonome-san!"

"Kuro!"

Suimei and I ran off in the direction she pointed and found Kuro, Tamaki-san, and—thank God—Shinonome-san, piled atop one another. I flung off Tamaki-san, the one on top, and shook Shinonome-san's unconscious body. By my side, Suimei was saying something to Kuro.

"Hey, do you really need to be that rough?" Tamaki-san grumbled, lying flat on the floor. "...Well, maybe I deserved it, hah."

He shut his eyes. His head was bleeding; it looked as though he had been hit by something hard.

I felt bad, but I left Tamaki-san be for now in order to prioritize Shinonome-san. "Shinonome-san, Shinonome-san! Wake up..."

I hugged my listless father tightly. I recognized his familiar smell, but he did not return the hug, nor even roughly make a mess of my hair. I became disheartened. "Why?! Why did you do this?!" I yelled at Yao Bikuni, giving way to my anger.

She smiled thinly and took a puff from her smoking pipe. The smoke she exhaled reflected off the little sunlight that shone into the cave, making it look as though threads were strewn about the darkness. "Why? Because I found him disagreeable, of course."

"What? Just what did he do to you?!"

"You fool. Think for yourself... That's what my unkind self wants to say, but today I'll make an exception and tell you just what he did. That man overstepped his bounds." She struck her smoking pipe against a nearby rock and grimaced with vexation. "He tried to destroy my world."

"What...?" I murmured.

With a distant look in her eyes, she said, "He's always been a strange man. He saved a human child and raised it. As a nun, I understand the sanctity of life and prefer to avoid senseless deaths, so I turned a blind eye."

"By human child, do you mean me...?"

"Yes. But in the end, it was an error to turn a blind eye to you. Because of you, the spirits grew docile, defanged. Oh, why do the spirits change so easily? Is the spirit realm not an unchanging world where the old can remain old? ...But that has nothing to do with me. Everyone can just do what they like for all I care...or so I thought."

She slowly pointed at Shinonome-san. "One day, that man came to me in search of information for a book he was making. He said he wanted to breathe new life into the spirit realm... Can you believe it?! Aha ha ha ha! I thought he had lost it!"

Come to think of it, Sojobo, the Great Tengu of Mount Kurama, had also said Shinonome-san visited him. Knowing Shinonome-san's passion for his book, I could see him making the rounds to every corner of the spirit realm for more stories. I doubted he had imagined visiting Yao Bikuni would backfire, though.

The smile disappeared from Yao Bikuni's face, and in a chilling voice, she said, "...He's such a bother." Her face was as placid as a Noh mask, but her words held thorns. "At the very least, I certainly don't desire such change. I've long since grown tired of it."

She reached into her breast pocket and pulled something out, holding it aloft. The sun was higher by now, allowing for more light to slip through the slit above. Thanks to that, I could catch a clear look of what she held in her hand. It was the missing half of Shinonome-san's main body, a piece of the torn hanging scroll. Her other hand held a lighter. Tensing her thumb, she flicked it on.

"Stop it, Yao Bikuni! Do you have any idea what you're doing?!" Noname yelled.

Yao Bikuni's cold gaze turned to her. With her patience running thin, she said, "So annoying. Of course I know what I'm doing! Now hand over the manuscript and promise me you won't try and publish that book, or I'll burn this. Surely you know what happens to a Tsukumogami when their main body disappears?"

The souls of Tsukumogami dwelled in the objects they originated from. The destruction of those objects meant the death of the Tsukumogami.

I trembled in fear and pleaded with her. "No! Please, don't hurt Shinonome-san any further!"

Her eyes shot open wide. Then she snickered softly before frowning sadly. "That, coming from the daughter of the man who tried to hurt *me*?"

Just then, something bright flew past me. It fluttered, shining with ghostly ephemeral light—a glimmerfly.

What was a glimmerfly doing here? Surprised, I momentarily forgot what was happening and let its radiance take my attention. As I did so, the surrounding area grew brighter all at once. I looked toward the source of the light and saw Yao Bikuni leaning against a large rock with a flock of glimmerflies gathering at her feet. No, that wasn't quite right. The glimmerflies weren't gathering at her feet—they were overflowing out of a gap between the ground and the rock.

"Ah, morning has come. The butterflies dreaming of the human world escape the cage that is the spirit realm once again." Yao Bikuni watched, detached from the world as though lost in a dream. Even more glimmerflies began to pour out of the earth, turning that part of the ground as bright as the midday sky—and dispelling the darkness of the cave.

"What the hell is that?" Suimei muttered. "Statues?"

With the light of the glimmerflies, we could now see stone statues lining the walls. I had thought they were just weird rocks earlier, but in truth, they were depictions of men and women, both old and young, all overlooking us. Their clothing and hairstyles varied, ranging from all kinds of time periods.

The glimmerflies perched on these statues, making them stand out against the darkness. We stood and stared at them in shock. That was when Yao Bikuni said, "That which doesn't change is best. Wouldn't you agree, Kaori? What is unchanging stays by your side forever, filling the holes of your heart, never leaving you and never being taken away."

She leaned against a particularly large statue, one of an elderly man. The statue wore an affectionate smile and held out its arms as though reaching forward to hug Yao Bikuni.

"No. These statues couldn't be..." I whispered.

"Yes, these are the ones who died and left me behind. I grew tired of parting from my beloved families over and over, so I made my own that would never leave me. Ridiculous, no?" Suddenly slumping with great exhaustion, she smiled. "Shall I continue Tamaki's story?

"I loved and I loved, and eventually I always ended up alone. After eight hundred years of repeating that same cycle, I grew tired of it. My tears had dried up long before I came to this cave to undergo nyujo. I had hoped fasting and chanting sutras would earn me the benevolence of Buddha, but it was not to be." She grimaced. "But of course it wouldn't. That wasn't the point of nyujo to begin with. No matter how many sutras I chanted, no end came for me. In that darkness absent of even a streak of light, as vermin crawled over my body, the only thing that came to me was loathing for my immortal self."

Once she understood nyujo was futile, she stopped chanting. But she made no effort to leave the cave, not wanting to build new relations with humans. Instead, on whim alone, she began carving the images of those she had once loved into stone. She had no tools, using only loose rocks to chip away at the stone. She would call their names, and once finished, caress their faces and embrace them. Those moments were precious to her.

"Every time I created a statue of one I had loved, my heart would somehow feel more whole. The feelings, the warmth, the voices, the memories—everything came back to me and warmed my heart. I couldn't see anything, but I was happy to know that I was surrounded by family again."

*Good morning. Are you hungry?*

*Remember that one time? We laughed so much, we doubled over, didn't we?*

*You'll catch a cold if you're not careful. Come here, Mommy will keep you warm.*

"But every now and then, it would all come crashing down in bouts of clarity. They never responded to me. They never had warmth to share with me. They never smiled back at me. Whenever I realized that, I became heartbroken. The unchanging family I had made could never truly make my heart whole! …And that left me in despair."

One day, as she chipped away at stone like on any other day, a glowing butterfly appeared from a rift in the rock. It fluttered gracefully through the air and illuminated its surroundings, displaying a phantasmal quality not of this mortal realm. It slipped through a crack in the ceiling that had formed some time ago and dissolved upon hitting sunlight.

Yao Bikuni had found the experience curious and begun digging down. She ignored her bleeding hands and ripping fingernails and continued to dig, more and more butterflies appearing as she did.

She was certain something lay deeper within, and she was proven right after years of digging, when an unknown world revealed itself before her.

"As astonishing as it is, an entrance to the spirit realm exists beneath this place. There, I found creatures living the old way of life…spirits. I was overjoyed, of course, as some of those spirits had lived eternities longer than even I."

She thought that maybe in their world, she could live without being hurt. At last she had found a world for her. A place she could live. A place where no one would leave her behind.

A place she could belong.

"I began to think that I could fall in love again if I did so there… True love, one that lasts for eternity. And as luck would have it, my body had changed into something inhuman over the years. I've become quite alike to the denizens of the spirit realm, wouldn't you think? That's why—" Her eyes widened, bloodshot, as she yelled, "—I won't forgive anyone who tries to destroy my world! The spirit realm doesn't need anyone to breathe new life into it! So hurry up and swear to me that you'll abandon your plans to make this foolish book!"

She held Shinonome-san's main body aloft again and lit the lighter. The glimmerflies scattered away from her, afraid of the flame.

I didn't know what to do and simply hugged my arms tight around Shinonome-san.

"I don't care... Do it."

Within my arms, I felt Shinonome-san stir awake and slowly open his eyes. I met his blue-gray eyes and smiled. But my joy was short-lived as the paleness of his face, the cracks along his skin, and the cold sweat that seeped into his clothes gave me too much to worry about.

Yao Bikuni froze and glared at him with seething hatred. "So you've finally decided to join us. Could you repeat yourself? I didn't quite catch what you just said."

"I said do it, Yao Bikuni. Burn that thing."

"Shinonome-san, no!" I pleaded.

"If that'll make you happy, then do it. But it won't stop me. I swear it."

"Please, don't..."

I didn't understand how he could say such things and pleaded with him to stop, but he didn't look my way. His eyes were locked squarely on Yao Bikuni.

Then, he somehow sat up with his weak body. "I've long since decided that I'll make my family happy with my writings."

Yao Bikuni laughed scornfully. "Ha ha ha ha! A hanging scroll Tsukumogami thinks he can be a writer? Was pretending to be a family with a human really that enjoyable? You know, I heard rumors about your main body in the human world... You're a cursed scroll that brings fortune at the cost of bloodshed. You've brought ruin to many up until now, and yet you think you deserve to live with a happy family? There are limits to any joke, you know."

"You're not wrong." Shinonome-san grinned wryly and rested his head on my shoulder. Even sitting seemed to be a struggle for him. His breathing was ragged, and more and more fissures appeared along his skin before my eyes. "It's been so long, I don't remember when exactly it was... But at some point in time, rumors that I brought fortune to those who owned me began to spread. There wasn't a bit of truth to it, but people believed it anyway, stealing me and sometimes being stolen from. I've been used as a tool by the government, and even had blood spilled upon me. Some time ago, I came to see humans as utterly foolish."

He hugged my shoulders and smiled, his pale face revealing pearly white teeth. "We're not too different. I grew tired of all the fighting around me and hid away in the spirit realm. I was fed up with humans and wanted to wash my hands clean of them. But then, one day...I adopted a human. A human that couldn't survive without me, a cute little crybaby of a girl. A small, weak thing that would cling to the hem of my clothes with her tiny, tiny hands."

His blue-gray eyes looked at me with genuine love from the bottom of his heart. "I thought that maybe I could grant someone *real* happiness for once, not the fake happiness I was rumored to bring. I may be a Tsukumogami just imitating human appearance and behavior, but I swore to make this girl happy." His gaze softened. "Because I am her father."

Yao Bikuni stared at Shinonome-san coldly and shook her head. "Spare me. All that has nothing to do with this."

"No, it does. I love my ever-changing daughter, and that makes me different from you." He touched my cheek with a trembling hand and wiped away my tears. "I know she'll pass away and leave me behind one day, and I'll be sad then, but I sure as hell won't regret anything. All I'll feel is the satisfaction and pride of knowing I raised her well."

"Sh-Shinonome-san..." I said through tears.

"Ah... You've always been such a crybaby. Don't cry. Everything's going to be all right, Kaori. I'm right here."

I hugged him tightly. Hot tears fell from my eyes, one after another, with no sign of stopping. Feelings of love and gratitude warmed my chest as a sense of happiness enveloped me. But at the same time, the fear that I would lose my father returned. Yao Bikuni still held my father's life in her hands. Knowing this, I hugged him even tighter—as though to beg for him not to be taken from me.

"Don't give me that," Yao Bikuni quietly whispered. My eyes shot up to her, fearful of the latent anger in her voice. But that fear faded when I saw the face she was making. She looked just like a child on the verge of tears after having her favorite toy taken away.

"You can only say that because you've never known what loss feels like!" she wailed. She relit the lighter and, without hesitation, brought it closer to the hanging scroll. "I was foolish. There's no point in being so roundabout when killing you will solve everything... You're an eyesore. Disappear."

"Stop it!" I yelled, just as a black shadow lunged toward her.

"Grrrr!"

"Ugh, get off me!"

It was Kuro. He had recovered consciousness and secretly drawn closer to Yao Bikuni. As he lunged, he bit her wrist.

I breathed a sigh of relief as I watched the lighter fall to the ground and the flame flicker out. Then, as though she didn't feel any pain, Yao Bikuni grabbed Kuro's neck and tore him away from her arm. "Damned...mutt!"

Kuro let out a yelp as he was harshly thrown to the ground. Yao Bikuni began searching the floor for the lighter. That was when Suimei made his move, pulling talismans out of his pocket and throwing them at her. The talismans seemed to stop midair for a moment—before flying toward her as though they had a mind of their own.

"Tch... No, stay away!"

The glimmerflies began to gather around Yao Bikuni like they were trying to protect her, blocking the talismans. But Suimei quickly reached into his pocket to pull out a vial and approached. She responded by extracting a smoking pipe from her breast pocket and whacking the back of his hand, causing the vial to fall and break on the floor. The liquid inside the vial splashed onto her leg, causing her to grimace as white smoke smoldered off of her.

A high-pitched voice called out, "Suimei, duck!"

Noname, who had approached from behind Suimei, swung a fist at Yao Bikuni. Suimei quickly ducked down.

From Yao Bikuni's perspective, Noname appeared out of thin air. Her punch landed unguarded, sending Yao Bikuni flying back. Noname then rubbed her fist with her other hand as she complained. "Owww! Goodness, that hurt. Are you trying to mar this porcelain skin of mine?!"

"What's the big deal? It's just skin."

"Oh, Suimei... You just don't understand a maiden's heart. You'll get dumped one of these days, as you are."

Noname's fist had swollen red. Just how hard did she have to punch for that to happen?

"Ngh..." Yao Bikuni had slammed into a stone statue. She tried to stand up but seemed to be unable to, perhaps because of a concussion. Shinonome-san's hanging scroll was still tightly clutched in her hand, and her eyes burned with a fiery will. That being said, it seemed to me that it would be hard for her to continue this fight. Her face was swollen from the punch, and her consciousness seemed fuzzy as her head bobbed slightly.

She spat out the blood in her mouth, and I heard something solid clack off the ground. A tooth had popped out.

"Yao Bikuni, please. Return Shinonome-san's main body,"

I pleaded, not wanting to see her hurt anymore. "Isn't this enough?! Let's end this already!"

But she just shook her head and, as her hand felt around on the ground, weakly smiled. "This pain is nothing compared to the possibility that the only place I belong will change. I won't die. I can't die. The curse of that mermaid meat won't let me die. That's why...I have to protect my world. I'm tired of losing people... No corner of my heart has been left unscarred."

She grimaced as though she would break into tears at any moment, but no tears fell. I thought that perhaps her tears had dried up long ago, like she said. That was when she raised the hand that had been feeling around the ground, now holding the lighter.

"Burn..." A small flame flicked on in her hand, and she brought it to Shinonome-san's main body.

"Ah—" It was all so sudden that I couldn't react.

The red flame spread to the hanging scroll and began to char the paper black. The smell of something burning reached me as Shinonome-san groaned lowly in my arms. Fearfully, I cast my gaze down and saw his skin char black. I wanted to scream, but no voice came out as I choked up instead. I put Shinonome-san down on the floor and ran at Yao Bikuni, still unsure of what I was going to do.

"Grrrrr!" At the same time, Kuro, now back on his feet, ran toward her with a growl. He used his tail like a whip and wrapped it around her wrist. Yao Bikuni dropped the lighter and struggled to break free of Kuro's tail. As a result, her attention was solely focused on him.

"Now, cat!" Kuro yelled.

Then suddenly, I heard a voice far too lax for the situation. "Humph. For a nun, you sure don't have many openings. You did well, mutt."

Nyaa-san appeared, slinking out of Yao Bikuni's shadow, in her enormous, post-transformation form. Her mismatched eyes twinkled. "Did you know, we carnivorous beasts like to hunt our prey by stalking in the shadows and waiting for them to let down their guard?"

She opened her jaw wide enough to swallow a human whole—drool dripping through the gaps of her vicious fangs—and bit into the left side of Yao Bikuni's body, tearing it off.

"Ugh, aaagghh!" Yao Bikuni let out an ear-piercing wail that echoed through the cave.

I heard the disgusting crunch of flesh being chewed and twitched involuntarily. A pool of fresh blood expanded outward from where Yao Bikuni fell on the ground.

Just as I thought Nyaa-san had swallowed, she spat something out right in front of me and grimaced. "Gross. Shinonome-san, you should give up smoking. The stink sticks to you."

"Ah..." I weakly fell to the floor. With some trepidation, I reached out for Shinonome-san's main body, the hanging scroll. The only actually burnt part was the paper framing the edges; the actual picture itself was unharmed. The flames had been snuffed out by Nyaa-san's mouth. Apart from some soot and blood stains, it seemed okay.

I slowly turned my gaze toward Shinonome-san, on the ground. He weakly raised his arm and gave me a thumbs up.

The corners of my lips pulled back into a smile, and I squatted down, hugging Shinonome-san's main body.

"Thank goodness..."

Relief surged from the depths of my heart as large beads of tears streamed down my face.

"Ah... You all got me good." Yao Bikuni vacantly looked up at the ceiling with her back on the ground.

Noon had snuck up on us. The light coming through the gap in the ceiling was blinding in comparison to the darkness of the cave. The countless glimmerflies of earlier had flown into the sunlight and dissolved before my eyes. I was surprised to learn that the glimmerflies were drawn to sunlight.

Yao Bikuni turned her eyes toward me and hoarsely said, "Why are you helping me?"

"Don't talk for now, please." I wiped the sweat off my brow with my bloodied hands and continued wrapping the dressing I'd borrowed from Noname around Yao Bikuni's body. "This should stop the bleeding, but you shouldn't move for a while. Noname will be back soon with some medicine that helps stimulate blood cell growth."

"Humph."

"I'm sorry my treatment is so basic, but Noname and Suimei refused to do it, so...yeah. But that's kind of your fault, so reflect on that a bit, okay?"

"Impertinent little..."

"Didn't I just say not to talk?" I said with a smile. "Oh, but this doesn't mean I've forgiven you or anything." I turned away with a huff.

"You act like a child. Ridiculous."

"You're one to talk. Act your age for once." I smiled wryly and wiped the blood off my hands, then sighed in relief.

I was pretty sure I had stopped the bleeding for now. It was pretty incredible that she could remain conscious after losing so much blood, but maybe that was just a perk of being immortal. She certainly didn't seem like she could just sprout a new arm anytime soon, but it was possible that she didn't actually need medicine at all, even in her state.

That being said, she was still missing the entirety of her left arm. It looked so painful that I couldn't bring myself to just leave her. Nyaa-san, who had eaten the arm, told Yao Bikuni it had tasted pretty all right, ranking her flavor above that of Shinonome-san's.

Tamaki-san and Shinonome-san had been carried back to the apothecary by Nyaa-san. The two of them were probably out of the woods by now, but it seemed it would take some time before they made full recoveries...

I started packing away the first aid kit I had borrowed from Noname. It was covered in blood now, so I wanted to find some water to clean it with.

Kuro seemed to pick up on this. "I'll go fetch some water!"

"Thank you, Kuro."

"Don't worry about it! I feel bad for not doing more earlier." With his tail wagging in the air, he ran off, carrying a bucket in his mouth.

*Kuro was always the happy-go-lucky one.* Then, out of the corner of my eye, I saw Suimei leaning against the cave wall with an unamused look on his face. *And Suimei was always the grumpy one...*

I grinned wryly. "Hey, don't you think it'd be all right to put those talismans away for now?"

"Don't be stupid," Suimei responded. "We don't know what this woman might do." He held talismans in his left hand and a vial of something in his right hand, positioned to be ready to fight at any moment.

With a smile, I sighed. "Whatever makes you happy."

Yao Bikuni muttered, "How can you smile like that? Don't you despise me?"

"Huh?"

"I tried to hurt someone precious to you. You should be acting like Noname, or that boy there. After what I did, I'd have no right to complain if that cat devoured me." She grimaced weakly. "Perhaps that would have been better."

I thought for a moment, carefully choosing my words. "I don't particularly hate you or anything."

"Hah! Don't be foolish. I don't need you to try to comfort me."

"I'm not, really. You've always looked out for me until now, telling me not to wear skirts and asking me if I'm eating my vegetables or doing my homework and such."

"You're saying I've been a nag?" she asked, somewhat sulkily.

"No, that's not it," I said with a smile. "I don't have anyone else in the spirit realm who tells me off like you do. Sure, there are people who say things to get under my skin, but you're the only one who says that kind of thing for my sake. Thank you."

She averted her eyes, so I continued. "You're kind, but also not kind. It's a weird thing to say, but I think it fits you to a tee. Though I am disappointed to see you hurt someone."

Yao Bikuni seemed to want to say something, hemming and hawing a bit, but ultimately she just shook her head and gave me a familiar line: "I am not so kind. Not one bit."

I sighed, exasperated. I rested my jaw on my knees and stared off into the cave. "You really are, though. Kinder than anyone else. Otherwise, your family here wouldn't be making such happy faces."

"What...?" Yao Bikuni looked at the stone statues, her face pained.

"You carved them by hand in the darkness, right? Then these must be the faces they made that you remembered best. Look, every one of them is so happy... The days they spent with you must have been happy ones."

Looking again, all the statues were rough and unpolished. But their expressions stood out and caught my eye regardless. A child smiling without a care in the world. A person with a heavily wrinkled grin. A mother proudly showing off the child in her arms. An old man brimming with love, his arm reaching.

"Normal people would be too scared to ever love another,

knowing they'll one day disappear, and yet, you've loved so many," I said. "Plus, I know what happened on that island. You let Suimei meet his mother. If you aren't kind, then what are you?"

Yao Bikuni didn't respond, simply staring at the stone statues. I watched her as I continued. "What you said earlier shocked me. Just imagining how it must've felt makes me choke up."

"What do you understand about me?" she said. "You haven't even married yet, much less had a child of your own."

I shook my head and pointed to the statues. "What choked me up was imagining how *they* must've felt, not you."

I looked around the cave and marveled again at just how many statues there were. I could never understand how Yao Bikuni had felt, watching each of their lives come to a close. But I could understand the pain of having to leave the one you loved behind.

"I'm sure they all wanted to stay with the one they loved till the very end..." I said, wondering what those who had lived alongside Yao Bikuni felt in their last moments... No, I really didn't have to wonder at all. The smiles carved on their faces left nothing to imagination. "...I'm jealous." The words were out of my mouth before I realized it.

Yao Bikuni scowled at me. "Are you joking right now?"

"Not at all. I mean it from the heart."

Unlike spirits, humans had a limited life span. That meant for us, death was something to fear. Not many could peacefully come to terms with it. Death was colder, darker, and crueler than all else. No matter how much we might beg it for mercy, it would come when our time was due. Death was our harsh, inevitable fate—and it was the reason why people hoped that they might be able to share their last moments with those they cherished most. People wanted to feel their loved ones' warmth and hear their gentle voices to dispel the fear of their final end.

There was nothing more frightening than a lonely death.

*"Kaori!"*

I imagined the smiling visage of my father's unkempt face and became a bit disheartened. At our core, humans are selfish creatures. Even if we know it will only burden others, we want our way, especially in regard to our death. We ignore the sadness our end will bring and beg our loved ones to stay with us.

Humans are weak. We can't live alone, and we can't die alone. The only thing we can give to those who stay with us in our final moments are our words.

"'Thank you,'" I said. "'I'm sorry,' 'I love you. Thanks for everything,'"

"What...?"

"If I were part of your family, those are the kinds of things I think I might say to you on my deathbed."

Yao Bikuni gasped, her eyes shooting wide open. Feebly, she propped herself up. "How?" She grabbed my clothes with her right hand and yelled, "How do you know the things they said?"

A single crystal-clear tear fell from her eye, soon followed by many more.

"Do you really understand how they felt? Ha ha... I can't believe it."

Her tears, which she claimed had dried up long ago, continued unabated and wet her bloodstained clothes. Her lip trembled. "They all thanked me in their final moments," she said weakly. "I just wanted someone to love. I was selfish. I knew they would die and hurt me one day, but I still loved them..." She clung to my hand, shook her head, and shut her eyes. "And yet they all smiled in the end! They thanked me. Why?! They didn't have a single reason to thank someone as selfish as me!"

Perhaps lacking the strength to support herself, Yao Bikuni fell. I quickly moved to catch her, ending up hugging her tightly. I patted her back as she sobbed and continued to ask herself "Why?" Eventually, she buried her face in my shoulder and entrusted her weight to me.

I looked up at the loving faces of the statues and consoled her, thinking carefully before I spoke. "Don't cry. Everything's...going to be all right."

"Uuaahh, aaaah..."

"They were just returning the love you gave them. There's nothing strange about it at all."

"Uuuah, aaah..."

"The change you feared wasn't that of the world but of yourself. You wanted to stay the same so the Yao Bikuni they loved would always exist."

"Uuaaaaaaaagh!"

That was why she never found another lover, even after coming to live in the spirit realm. Perhaps her old family was also the reason why she looked after the recuperating souls. On the off chance one of them appeared there, she could do everything in her power to save them. Just like how Suimei did for his mother.

I knew it. Yao Bikuni was kind. There was no greater wife or mother than this spirit. Her love ran deeper than any other's, but it also weighed on her.

I continued to speak, perhaps more for my sake than hers. "It's all right. The love those people felt for you won't change, even if you do. So please...forgive those who went first and left you behind. Forgive yourself for being able to do nothing but watch from their side. Only gods can stave off death. The world...is not so kind. There are no miracles. We have to accept the inevitable ends that come."

Yao Bikuni slowly raised her face. She looked at me with her teary eyes, and her smile was conflicted. "Why...are you crying as well?"

"Aha ha..." I didn't bother wiping away the tears streaming down my face. "I was just thinking that the world would be such a nice place if it were as full of miracles as in stories... But it isn't, so I just somehow ended up crying."

She gave me a troubled smile and began wiping away my tears with the hem of her sleeve. "Oh, don't cry. I'm not so good with this soppy stuff... Even though I was the one bawling just moments ago."

"S-sorry."

"You're much too young to be saying such hopeless things, anyway. Miracles are miracles because they only rarely occur. We wouldn't appreciate them otherwise." She began to fix my disheveled hair and clothes as she muttered faintly. "You being here is a miracle in itself... You taught me something I've been struggling to understand for a long time."

"Huh? I did?" I asked, to which she snickered softly.

"It's fine if you don't know," she said with a far-off look in her eyes. She let out a deep, tired sigh. "In the end, I was just looking for a target for my anger... What happened to me wasn't anyone's fault. There isn't anyone to blame or to forgive. This is simply the world we were born to."

The soft smile she gave me then left me astonished. It was the smile of a mother who had raised many children, the smile of a young girl whose heart was aflutter, and the smile of an elderly woman who had lived many years with her loved one. I saw the eight hundred years' worth of time Yao Bikuni had lived all overlaid atop one another, carved into a single smile.

"What a handful you are, child. To think you would even change me..." she whispered as she brought my head to her chest. Gently, she began to pat my back. "This world isn't so kind. But the people in it are."

With her arm wrapped around me, she began to rock as though lulling a child to sleep.

*One-two-three, one-two, one-two...*

"Ah..." I murmured.

The rhythm of her rocking was broken, perhaps due to her injuries. It was the same rhythm of Shinonome-san's rocking in my childhood.

My heart was touched by the familiar sway as one last tear fell from my eye.

# A Promise
# Between Family

T HE INCIDENT in Yao Bikuni's meditation cave came to an end, and we returned to our everyday lives.

Shinonome-san and Tamaki-san's injuries continued to heal, and they kept themselves busy with publishing preparations. In the end, Shinonome-san decided to forgive Yao Bikuni.

"I kind of understand how she felt," he said with a slightly sad look on his face.

Yao Bikuni, now without a left arm, returned to looking after the recuperating souls. Something seemed to have changed within her however, as I heard through the grapevine that more souls had been saved as of late.

Part of me still couldn't forgive her. But after learning how she felt, I just couldn't bring myself to hate her. I decided I would treat her like I had before, with just a bit of extra caution. She seemed to do the same, giving me the usual embarrassing scolding whenever I delivered books. She would occasionally make a face now and then, but ultimately, we were back to the way things had been. It seemed to me that the incident had given us a mutual understanding that our relationship was one of those things that just didn't need to change.

There were things that changed, things that didn't change, and things that could never be changed. Only by perfectly balancing the three could one live their best life.

The end of autumn neared, and signs of the coming winter began to appear.

Cold winds shook the glass of the windows. It was still a bit too early to pull out the heater, but it was just cold enough to bring out the hibachi brazier.

"Shinonome-san, congratulations on the release."

"Oh, thanks!"

"Don't drink too much now. At least wait for everyone else to show up first."

"I know, I know."

He poured the high-grade Japanese sake I had splurged on into his favorite sake cup, filling it until only surface tension held it in and sipping off anything above the edge.

Tomorrow was the long-awaited release of his book. We would be lending it out at our bookstore, naturally, as well as selling it to those who wanted their own copy. But before that, we were having a party to celebrate the book's release.

Shinonome-san's dream was soon to be realized.

"Kaori, is this the last of the food?"

"Oh, yeah. Thanks, Suimei."

Suimei brought over a big plate of food from the kitchen, specially made for today, but...

"Everyone's late..." Even after the scheduled time, nobody showed up. Tired of holding back, Shinonome-san had begun drinking alone.

The winds shook the windows again. With the autumn leaves fallen, the trees outside looked cold and barren. I hadn't seen many spirits flying about in the air lately, given this chill, and I'd hardly seen any beast-type spirits anywhere at all, as they'd started cooping up in their homes. A prime example of the latter was the ball of fur in my house's corridor.

"Ugh... Heavy... Run away...Suimei..."

"Zzz... Zzz... Myah?! ...Zzz..."

Nyaa-san and Kuro were sleeping together as one big clump of black fur. It was quite amusing, as you couldn't tell where one began and the other ended, so it looked like they were some strange cat-dog chimera.

The two seemed so chummy as they slept, you wouldn't have thought they bickered like they did. Then again, their relationship had changed after the fight with Yao Bikuni. No, maybe changed was saying too much... Nyaa-san had merely come to see Kuro just a tad bit more favorably than before, and Kuro was no longer constantly running away from Nyaa-san. The difference really was slight. Only those who dealt with them often, like me, could tell there was even a difference at all. Still, it was a welcome change.

Every now and then, Kuro's front paws would twitch into action, and he would let out a pained whine. I imagined it was because Nyaa-san was riding up on his body, disturbing his sleep.

"Should we move Nyaa-san?" I asked Suimei.

"Nah. If Kuro really hated it, he'd move himself."

"Uh-huh..."

I had Suimei pegged as the overprotective type, but he surprisingly trusted Kuro to make his own choices. A chuckle escaped me as I walked over to the kitchen to get enough plates for everyone who would be coming. That was when I heard some voices from the entrance.

"Oh dear, it's so chilly outside! And it isn't even winter yet! Now I'm all late because of it."

"No, we're late because you couldn't find your fur coat and had to upend your room to find it!"

"Yeah. Why'd we have to help with that again?"

It was Noname and the Kinme-Ginme twins. The three of them noisily entered the house and crowded into the living room.

"Sorry we're late, dears," Noname said. "Congratulations on the release, Shinonome. I've brought along some well-cured sake I've been setting aside for a day like this!"

"Gramps gave us some green pheasant meat to give y'all. Let's get some hot pot going!" Ginme said.

"I'm going to borrow the kitchen for a bit, Kaori. I brought some tofu from Kyoto," Kinme said.

Another guest arrived soon after.

"Congratulations on the release, Shinonome. You know, I've

been thinking this for a while now, but the way you're going from book-lending to publishing is kinda like you're following in the footsteps of Kamakura Bunko, yeah? I think that's pretty incredible! As your friend, I'm proud of you."

This arrival with a stylish mustache and a brand-name suit was Toochika-san, the kappa spirit who ran a store in Kappabashi, Tokyo. He had used his business connections in the human world to help get Shinonome-san's book printed.

He took off his hat to reveal a plate on his head, which he rubbed anxiously as he said, "While the publishing itself is going without a hitch...we need to have a serious conversation about how we're going to avoid the pitfalls Kamakura Bunko fell into. Now, you're no Kawabata Yasunari, nor does your book include any short stories by Mishima Yukio or anything by Endo Shusaku, but... Ah, we're doomed. We're going to go bankrupt just like Kamakura Bunko!"

"Oh, be quiet, you," Shinonome-san said. "Why are you making it sound like we're doomed to fail before we even start? Those guys aren't even around anymore!"

Toochika-san let out a jovial laugh, then sat next to Shinonome-san and began discussing business.

I smiled at the familiar scene. More people soon arrived, making the room feel even more cramped than before.

"Congratulations! Here, make sure you eat this."

"I can't wait to read the book! I'm in it too, right?"

"Hey, I got a distant relative saying they want to be in your next book!"

Spirits from around the neighborhood, long-time customers of the store...and just ordinary passersby gathered inside, all congratulating Shinonome-san with big smiles. Shinonome-san had his hands full just trying to thank them all. I noticed, however, that there was a person who should have been there who was missing—someone who had worked just as hard as Shinonome-san to make this book a reality, and who was therefore fully deserving of these congratulations.

I sneaked out of the store, into the street, and scanned the area. I found Tamaki-san leaned up against a wall by himself. He had an incredibly gaudy scarf around his neck, and his nose was red and sniffling. Through his sunglasses, I could see his eyes unhappily shut.

"There you are. Everyone's waiting for you, c'mon," I said.

He scoffed. "Waiting for me? Please. I'm well aware that nobody would want me to ruin their celebration; I'm doing you all a favor by sitting this one out. Nobody likes being forced to read a story they don't like, now do they?"

"You're as cryptic as ever... Just get in, who cares. It's cold outside."

"Ha ha. You're unyielding, but I suppose I should expect such from the daughter of Shinonome." He turned on his heel and waved. "Unfortunately, I have other business to take care of and will have to decline."

"Oh... Like what?"

"Little miss, have you not noticed? Somebody's been scheming behind the scenes of our recent debacle."

My eyes opened wide, but I wasn't sure of what he was getting at. Tamaki-san turned his head and peered at me with his white, clouded right eye.

"Who told the nun that Shinonome's main body was beneath the bookstore? To go ever further, who gave the nun's father that souvenir from the Palace of the Dragon King? Mermaid meat can easily make a mess of a human's life, yet that man so carelessly gave it away... Just who was he?" For the first time ever, the ever-aloof Tamaki-san showed me true anger.

"I've been searching for that man for a long, long time," he continued. "I even play the buffoon in my attempts to catch him. As such, I don't have time to waste on celebrations and the like."

"Just what did that man do to you?" I asked.

"Now, wouldn't you like to know?" Tamaki-san began walking off without explaining further. He waved as he went. "Give Shinonome my regards."

"Wait, where are you going? You'll come by again some time, right?" I asked, not wholly sure why I did so myself. I just had this nagging feeling Tamaki-san was going somewhere far, far away.

He stopped and, without turning around, said, "You should take a page from that young man's book, little miss. Don't let your guard down around me. Depending on how you interpret things, I may one day become your enemy. It'd be wise to keep your distance."

"No way!"

"What?" Tamaki-san spun around, looking utterly flummoxed by my instant reply. Perhaps he was just putting on airs to try and depart while looking cool, but I was having none of it.

"I haven't forgotten that time I went to Okinawa to deliver books. You gave us the information I needed to fulfill both that Kijimuna girl's dream and her father's. There was that time with Yao Bikuni too... You told us about her terrible life beforehand so we wouldn't assume that she was just a bad person."

"You're free to interpret what I say as you like."

"But if you never said any of that in the first place, things would likely have ended differently. Besides, while you often say I'm free to interpret things however I like, you never forget to leave a clear path that lets everyone be happy. I know you're a good person, Tamaki-san, and I'll continue to believe you are one from here on out."

Tamaki-san's eyes seemed to moisten a bit as he made a face like that of a child trying to hold back tears—but only for the briefest of moments. He let out a grandiose sigh and lowered the brim of his hat with his left hand. "...Do what you like. I am but a story-seller, and depending on the listener, a story can be wicked or virtuous. When the time comes, I hope you'll be careful as to how you interpret mine."

He lowered his head and smiled. "...I'm sure Shinonome will try writing another book again. I'll make sure to drop by to collect his manuscript then."

With a flutter of his haori, he left, coolly disappearing from the town.


After seeing Tamaki-san off, I returned to the shop and was immediately snagged by Shinonome-san. Perplexed, I was dragged into the crowded living room, where I realized everyone had a glass in hand. Shinonome-san thrust a glass of juice into my hands, then looked over everyone and cleared his throat.

"Ahem, thank you all for gathering here today. I am filled with joy to be able to release this book... It would seem a certain story-seller is missing from our celebration, but you'll have to forgive him, as he's a shy one."

A roar of laughter swept through everyone. A brief smile came to Shinonome-san's face but was soon replaced by a stern expression.

"This book is an unprecedented first for the spirit realm... Honestly, I don't know if it'll do well at all, but my hope is that it'll lead to the creation of many more books throughout our realm. Books enrich the heart and expand worlds—both the real world and the world of the mind. There are no limits to the worlds that can be created with books. I think they're genuinely incredible."

He smiled a bit from embarrassment and continued. "I'd be happy if my book could expand someone's world. Um, anyway, I owe everything to my daughter here today."

"Huh?" I looked up at him, surprised.

"Without her help, none of this would be possible," he said, a bit proudly. "I owe her a lot for helping me achieve my dream and want to repay the favor somehow. So, I swear from this day forward, I'll continue putting out more spirit realm-original books and make my daughter the happiest girl in the whole spirit realm. Of course, you all will help me, right?"

"There he goes, talking about his daughter again!" somebody groaned.

"And I won't ever stop talking about her! She's the cutest daughter in the world!" Shinonome-san replied. He took the ensuing heckling from everyone with a smile.

I was red in the face, with tears ready to stream down the moment I let my guard down. Shinonome-san then gave me a toothy grin and tousled my hair messily. He faced everyone with a wide grin. "I'm gonna do my best to become a father Kaori can be proud of and hope to have your help. Cheers!"

"Cheers!" the crowd echoed.

"Congratulations!"

"Good luck, Shinonome dear!" said Noname. "I'll be cheering you on!"

"You better meet those deadlines, you hear?!" said Toochika-san.

"Sorry, I can't make any promises there," replied Shinonome-san.

"Aha ha ha ha!"

Laughter filled the room. I took a small sip of my juice and glanced out the window.

"Ah..."

Thick clouds blanketed the sky, and white snow fell to the ground—the sign of an early winter. It had to be cold outside, and it would only get colder yet. Winter was a season of waiting, waiting for the warmth of spring to release us from the piling snow.

But at this moment, the cold of the outside world went unfelt as the room was warmed by the excitement of the spirits that filled it.

I smiled and gazed at Shinonome-san's back. He had accomplished his dream and was now setting off to achieve a new one.

I made a new wish: *Please let me remain this man's daughter.* Even if we weren't bound by blood, I wanted to be the best daughter I could be to support him.

I put a hand to my now warm chest and smiled, then joined in the fun with everyone else.

# The Curious Dog and the Dishonest Cat

THE PARTY WAS GOING STRONG in the bookstore.

Out in the corridor, a black cat slept. She opened a lone eye and let out a grand sigh. "They're so noisy. How am I supposed to sleep like this?" The success of the bookstore proprietor meant nothing at all to the Kasha spirit.

Few things were worthy of her attention: the daughter of the bookstore owner, canned cat food, sunny spots for a midday nap, the smell of human corpses, and a particular dog spirit—the one that so happened to be pinned underneath her right this very moment.

"Ngh... You're heavy, cat. Mind moving?"

"Huh? Did you just call me *heavy*? Have you never heard of tact, you mutt?"

"Ow, ow! Don't bite my ear!"

The black cat finally hopped off the Inugami and met his teary gaze with a glare before unapologetically turning away with a huff.

The Inugami—a dog spirit partnered with the former exorcist Suimei—was called "mutt" by the black cat, as the very sight of him irritated her. Every time she saw him happily walking alongside his owner, so blithe and carefree, she felt disheartened, as it was like she was looking at her past self.

With a flick of her tail, the black cat looked over at Kaori, currently noisily partying away together with Shinonome. The girl had looked so troubled up until just recently, yet she now wore such a worry-free smile. The black cat narrowed her eyes in contentment, genuinely happy for the girl.

"You really like her, huh?"

Her mood was soon dashed by the half-wit beside her, however. She spun around to look at the one who had made the inane comment, only for the Inugami's head to suddenly plop down atop her body.

"You're heavy. Move," she demanded.

"You're kidding! There's no way my head alone is that heavy! Besides, you were on me with your whole body earlier. It's only fair that I get back at you some." The Inugami's ears twitched as he laughed like a human might.

"Don't get cocky, mutt."

"I'm not. C'mon, we're both partnered to humans. Let's get along."

The Inugami was more assertive with the black cat after they'd worked together in the fight against Yao Bikuni. He hadn't cowered from her since.

*This is no fun. I prefer having him run away from me with his tail between his legs...* The black cat was dissatisfied, in part due to having lost a vital source of entertainment, but also because... "Partnered, huh..." she muttered.

She had no intent to partner with anyone.

"I'm Kaori's best friend and housemate," she said. "I don't butter up to her like a dog, so don't lump me together with you."

For some reason beyond her, the Inugami snickered.

"What's so funny?" she challenged him with a fierce glare.

After having his fill of laughter, the Inugami said, "They're the same thing! Partner, best friend... Either way, you're there to support each other when either of you are feeling down. No difference at all." He licked his own nose before continuing. "Cats are pretty funny. I don't care what I am as long as I get to be with Suimei, but I guess cats do."

The black cat soured at this. In a low voice, she muttered, "What the hell do you know? You don't know the first thing about me."

The Inugami's face instantly brightened, and without hesitation, he drew close to the black cat's face. Nearly touching noses, he said, "Then tell me. What things you like, how you became friends with Kaori—everything."

"Unbelievable. What brought this on?"

"Well, I've only seen you as this super scary monster up until recently, but Suimei said that not knowing about other people is what leads to baseless fear, so I want to get to know you better. Besides, there's also...that. Look." The Inugami pointed with his nose at two smiling humans, who had at some point moved closer to each other. "We'll definitely be involved with one another for a good long while, so we might as well get to know each other."

The black cat glared at the dog for a few moments before letting out a deep, weary sigh. She looked out the window and saw the white snow just beginning to fall. "...Fine. I'll tell you once it gets colder. Not like there's much to do in winter, anyway."

The Inugami's expression lit up, and he licked the black cat's nose. "He he he! Oh boy, I can't wait!"

"Meow?! What're you doing?!"

"I can't wait to be friends with a cat!"

"Meow?!" The black cat grimaced and popped the sharp claws out of her small feet. "Didn't I tell you not to get cocky?!"

Holding nothing back, she clawed at the Inugami.

# Afterword

THANK YOU for reading *The Haunted Bookstore – Gateway to a Parallel Universe – The Fake Family and a Promise Made Under the Stars*. I'm happy we could meet again.

This second volume featured a lot more formerly human spirits than the first. Generally speaking, these spirits lost their humanity against their will while retaining their human sensibilities. I was curious what kind of problems those kinds of spirits might face and ended up writing this book. But let's not forget, even these former humans are a type of spirit. I hope this book was able to remind you that spirits are things we fear and grieve, as well as sometimes pity.

Now then, as evident by the book's subtitle, the spotlight of this book is right on Shinonome and Kaori. Fathers seem to play a disproportionately high role in my works. I suppose it's because I myself love my father very much.

I used to be a daddy's little girl when I was little. I remember him like it was yesterday: the smell of tobacco; his broad back, large hands, and gentle gaze; the way he would sing that one children's song, "Hato Popo," in the evening on our walks. Sadly, he passed away while I was still young.

Maybe that's why I still remember him so vividly. I'm married now, but every now and then, whenever I'm having some trouble, I find myself thinking, "Ah, if only he were alive..."

Every time I see a beautiful evening sun, I'm reminded of those walks I went on with my father. I'm reminded of that world dyed red by the sunset and the slightly out-of-tune song my father would sing. It comes to me so keenly.

While it's not the only reason, it's definitely a part of why I want Kaori and Shinonome to be such a happy family. As luck would have it, I'm the author, so I get to make it happen, ha ha.

Moving along, I have some people I would like to thank. To my editor, Sato—thank you for all your praise. Please keep the praise coming, if you don't mind; I'm someone who does better the more praise I get, ha ha.

To Munashichi, thank you for the wonderful book cover art. You managed to take my nonsensical descriptions and make them reality! Truly amazing.

From the bottom of my heart, I am happy I wrote this book. Thank you all so much.

I'm also pleased to announce that the series is getting a manga adaptation drawn by Medamayaki! They also did the manga for one of my other series, *Isekai Omotenashi Gohan*. It's an honor to have them again! I can't wait!

THE CURIOUS DOG AND THE DISHONEST CAT

I'll be working my hardest to finish the next volume and get it into your hands. Please look forward to it. Until next time, take care.

Written in the second year of the Reiwa Era,
Shinobumaru